The Psychographist

"*The Psychographist* is an engrossing "stranger comes to town" tale that resonates like Stephen King and Bret Easton Ellis. Winter masterfully creates tension and dread from the mundane reality of modern life."

—Laird Barron author of *Not a Speck of Light*

"In *The Psychographist*, Carson Winter maintains his commitment to writing the most uncomfortable stories possible. In the vein of Needful Things, this is a deeply transgressive, bleak, and perverse narrative that compels you to read it even as you are repulsed, mirroring the behavior of the novel's doomed characters. Winter examines the ways in which happiness and desire are twisted by capitalism into near-cosmic experiences, and asks what it truly means to live in a world where our data is more valuable than our lives."

—Jolie Toomajan, Editor of *Aseptic* and *Faintly Sadistic*

"With sneaking apocalypticism and a hefty dose of well-earned paranoia, Carson Winter creates a vision of contemporary consumerism and terror that strikes at the heart of what it means to be trapped in the possessive darkness of 21st century capitalism. Poignant, provocative, and prescient, *The Psychographist* sees a bold new voice in horror fiction beginning to come into his power."

—Kurt Fawver, author of *We are Happy, We are Doomed*

"If I had a nickel for every time Winter pulled the rug out from under my feet, I'd have a deep pile of metal to fall into. You can reliably count on his wonderfully cynical mind to lead you down paths hidden behind menacing tapestries. He threatens the reader with every compelling sentence. Sometimes he follows through, sometimes you get out alive. I'm still not sure in which state *The Psychographist* has left me."

—Christopher O'Halloran, editor of *Howls from the Wreckage*

"A demented tale of consumerism run amok on the human psyche. A cosmic horror ode to our basest and most materialistic desires. An over-the-top satirical splatterfest that is as thought provoking as it is disgusting. What the fuck did I just read?"

—Danger Slater, author of *I Will Rot Without You*

THE
PSYCHOGRAPHIST

GARSON WINTER

Apocalypse Party

Cover Design & Typesetting by Mike Corrao

Paperback: 978-1-954899-12-4

A NOTE FROM THE AUTHOR

Some people will tell you that marketing isn't any one thing. They will claim, between gasping breaths, that it contains multitudes. They are right. These people make a living off of selling you SEO as self-help, PPC ads as spiritual confirmation. They live and breathe it; they eat it up and shit it out so that you can also eat it up and shit it out. These people worship it.

Marketing here is a force of fate. If sales are bad, it's marketing. If sales are good, it's marketing. This attributive necessity stretches far beyond the board room. For these people, marketing is a lifestyle. If someone doesn't want to fuck you on a dating app, it means you didn't market yourself correctly. If your parent dies, it means that the cosmic hand of market positioning deemed this to be the Ultimate Terminus, the long-awaited finale after a stretch of diminishing returns.

Critics will tell you that it's how a product is forcibly shoved down a wanton populace's throat. The wanton populace will tell you it's the ads on TV—the ones they ignore while taking a piss. The aforementioned zealots will tell you that it's *so much more*. Invariably though, *so much more* falls into one of four categories. Young peddlers know them as the four Ps.

Product, Place, Promotion, and Price.

We all know the product. It's the insurance that the erudite gecko tells us will save us money. Or, for a quaint period of time, it was a caveman.

1

Whatever whimsical figure presents it, we all know that they're selling us a product. It can be big or small, tangible or intangible. It can be the sort of thing that saves our lives, makes us hard, makes us pretty, or sits in a drawer until our survivors are forced to sort through our clutter. Whatever the product is, it is.

Then, there's place. This is where you get the product. Look closely next time a talking animal asks you if you need insurance. Is there a website? Is there a store? This is where your product resides, where your customer can traverse the dark and stormy whatever to get what they *need*. Wal-Mart, Amazon, your friend's Etsy—these are all places.

You can also think of place as the beginning of a hero's journey—that ancient story structure that serves as the skeleton for Star Wars, Harry Potter, and Gilgamesh alike. This is the customer's hero journey, where they travel to the underworld, with their card in hand, and come out victorious. They arrive back in their homestead carrying the product by its wild hair as it bleeds violently from the neck. The customer has won. They have hunted and gathered. They went to the place.

Promotion is what's carved into every surface we rest our eyes on. The word gets out and it never stops. It circles from person to person like a virus. There is no safety from promotion. This very book you're reading—how did you hear about it? Was it a recommendation? A Goodreads review? Did the algorithm on your favorite book-buying platform push the pretty cover right in front of your eyes? To acknowledge promotion is to acknowledge a lack of free will. That the world over is absent of decision making, that people are not made for original thought. Instead, they are machines activated by opportunity. We see the bait, we chomp down, we swallow happily.

But really, how often does it come down to the price?

Every time.

The answer is every time. The price defines the lengths we go to capture our product. For the right price, anything is worth it.

These four Ps make up what we call the Marketing Mix. But it is really only the beginning. There is more of course. There are funnels and SWOT analyses. There are channels and there are calls to action. But the most important part of this is you.

That's where we enter the world of people. It is people who feed this ghastly engine.

There is a field of study called psychographics that aims to study the human consumer. It lists your likes and dislikes, analyzes your patterns and motivations. Psychographics is the tarot reading of the 21st century. It is where we decide *who* buys the product. What kind of person needs this *thing*. What kind indeed. Somewhere, there is a consumer persona of you—exacting and insightful.

May you never have to witness its unvarnished reflection.

PLAGE

PURGE

ONE

"I don't think you can get pussy in that," said Grady.

"How would you know?" Cossel outlined the car in the magazine, tracing his fingers around the image, price, and description. "The choice isn't between this car and that car, it's between this car and no car."

Cossel and Grady were two teenage boys with brown hair, and if you didn't look closely, you could easily confuse them. Grady was taller, by an inch and a half, and had a squatter face. Cossel's features were longer, giving him the illusion of height. Together, they sat in Grady's room saying much the same things.

Grady chuckled—a weak, insecure thing. "Fair. But it's still a shit heap."

"It'll be *my* shit-heap though."

"Every knight needs his steed. You can be the brown knight with the shit-heap steed."

"And I'll ride her proudly into battle."

Grady had failed his first driver's test and had yet to retake it. A sore spot of which Cossel was well aware.

Grady rolled off the bed. "You're the type that would too."

"What's that supposed to mean?"

Grady picked up his guitar, an electric monstrosity with more points than strings, and strummed a chord. "Nothing, forget it. You going to Kayla's tonight?"

"What's happening at Kayla's?"

"A little get together."

"Anyone I know gonna be there?"

Grady shrugged. "I don't know. Kayla's parents are chill though. They're one of those 'I don't care if you drink, as long as you do it here,' types."

He closed the magazine. "Sure," he said. "Why not?"

Grady and Cossel had been friends since junior high, where they both ran track. In high school, they both quit when the expanded talent pool left them near the bottom of the rosters. Now, their conversations had become demonstratively masculine. They talked about cars and girls. They traded venomous barbs. Sometimes they talked about guys whose asses they were pretty sure they could kick. Other times, they reveled in the bodies of male fitness models, joyously explaining in exquisite detail how so-and-so could beat *their* ass. This was a sort of sacrifice. What had been given by testosterone must also be taken by it. Bowing before shredded movie stars was their exercise in humility, and in some ways, the prospect of being broken down by a god was as appealing as cracking another kid's nose with a flying knuckle.

Before they left, Grady kissed his mom on the cheek. "You boys are gonna be good now, right?"

"Yes, ma'am," said Grady.

And just like that, they were off.

There are forty-one Springfields in the United States. This one was as unspectacular as the rest. It was a medium-sized town that could be called a city by those who lived in small-sized towns. Those who lived in large-sized towns would scoff at the notion of this Springfield being a city, but that's how it goes. Its green population signs claimed 41,062 people—so, you be the judge.

Of those 41,062, there was Cossel and Grady and 41,060 more like them. Some of them were older or younger; some of them had different beliefs; but by and large, they were a ho-mogenous sort. Springfield sat at the confluence of two rivers and was populated with all the usual assortments one would find in small cities. Starbucks, McDonald's, strip malls, car lots, schools; red-brick downtowns filled with coffee shops, brew-pubs, and office buildings. It was the sort of playground that many parents dreamed of—an echo of their own childhood. Turmoil was unlikely to hit Springfield, and if it did, it was only a weak echo. Maybe it was the surrounding mountains, the hills, that blocked out the rest of the world.

It would be a mistake though to say that its population was provincial. The people here did not live with their heads buried any more than anyone else did. They were neither rural nor urban. If asked, they would consider themselves normal.

At sunset, the sky burst in a cosmic blast of pink and or-ange, black clouds twisted between rays of light. Pollution from the paper mill refracted and colored the sleepy sun in an extrav-agant rainbow. Springfield, like many places, could be beautiful.

Cossel stood a step behind Grady, who rang the doorbell. A pretty blonde girl answered, braces molten in the sunset.

"You made it," she said. She looked past Grady to Cossel, who subconsciously puffed out his chest. "Nice to see you made it."

"No problem," he said, unsure what he was supposed to say.

"Come on back," she said. "Everyone is hanging by the pool."

"Are your parents home?"

"No, they're out for the night."

"Cool," said Grady.

She led them through a house that looked like something out of a magazine. Cossel felt a pang of envy, but it was assuaged by the knowledge that Grady likely felt the same inferiority. Kayla's parents were loaded—a lawyer/doctor power couple that were by all accounts very nice too. Cossel hated that most of all. If you were rich, the least you could do was be mean too.

Outside, three other teenagers sipped on wine coolers. Two girls in bikinis stretched out on lawn chairs, as if their skin was thirsty for the last hour of sun. A boy—tall, muscular, and dark-haired—swam in the pool.

Kayla said, "This is my friend Grady and his friend, Cossel. Guys, meet Erica, Claire, and Dom."

Erica, a brunette with heart-shaped sunglasses said, "Pleased to meet you, boys." She said the final word with a bit of Aubrey Hepburn flair, vocal fry and transatlantic affect.

Claire adjusted her septum and said, "Welcome to the party," like the joke was that this wasn't a party at all.

Dom dived down to the bottom of the pool, came back up, and shook the water from his thick head of curly hair. Finally, in his own time, he asked, "What are you guys drinking?"

"Whatever you have," said Grady.

Dom pointed a finger at Cossel. "And you?"

"Ditto."

"My guys."

Kayla said, "We have a cooler over here. Between Erica and Claire. Help yourself, grab a seat. I'll get some music playing."

"Sounds good," said Cossel.

They sat in plastic chairs and each grabbed a beer—the least effeminate option—sipping forcefully, if not credibly, while making conversation about school and who knew who and how.

"Dom goes to Lincoln Heights."

"We're at Webster."

"How do you know Kayla?"

Claire said, "Old youth group friends."

Erica nodded. "We used to be all about God and shit. *All* about it."

Dom climbed out of the pool and sat between Claire and Erica. "Don't you still go?"

Kayla shook her head no. "No. Not anymore. But I still keep in touch with a lot of people."

There was a lull in conversation and Cossel felt a pleasant buzz. Deep inside of him, there was a sudden urge to share. Every secret thought he kept inside threatened to spill. He swallowed. Grady's cheeks were red, and his eyes were droopy. He wondered if he was also holding on for dear life.

Dom laid back on the concrete between the two young women. He too was drunk, although more practiced. He did not say anything stupid or make exaggerated movements. Instead, his eyes drooped lightly. The sky had darkened to the color of gunmetal.

"Have you ever been up there, Kayla?"

When Dom spoke, a wave of relief flowed through Cossel. He was afraid of what he might say if the silence went too long.

Kayla shook her head. "The roof? No. Of course not."

Claire and Erica laughed. Erica said, "You see something you like?"

"I guess," said Dom. He stood up and Cossel felt eerily on edge. Dom pointed to the roof, seeming to measure it with his gaze, then pointed to the pool. "Do you think we could make it in, if we jumped?"

All of them craned their necks to see. There was about ten feet of clearance from the edge of the roof to the pool.

"No way," said Kayla.

"Maybe," said Claire. "You'd have to really get going."

"I could do it," said Grady. "Definitely. Not even a problem."

"You're insane."

Dom smiled. "I'll go if you go."

The girls clapped, shrieking in joy. Kayla said, "My dad has a ladder."

She left in a hurry, Dom following her. Before long, as promised, they arrived with a ladder.

"I'm not doing it," said Cossel. "There's no way."

Grady drank his beer. "It'll be fine. The pool's right there."

"We're not dressed for it."

"It's water, dipshit. Who cares?"

Cossel scratched his hairless chin.

"You gonna puss out?" asked Claire.

Erica laughed, then took a long sip of her wine cooler.

"I didn't want to do it in the first place," said Cossel. "Grady can do it. I don't want to."

Dom was halfway up the ladder. "Don't let them bully you into it," said Dom. "Some people are just pussies."

Before Cossel could respond, Dom had already made it up to the roof. There was no wait time, no lead up. Dom jumped within seconds. Three steps and suddenly he was floating.

They all watched him. The boy was suspended.

And then the water exploded.

"See?" said Grady. "It's fine. He made it." He pulled his phone from his pocket, along with his wallet and house keys, placing them carefully on the table. "If you fuck with my shit, I'm gonna know," he said.

"I'm not doing shit."

Soon, Grady was up the ladder too. He stood on the roof, striking a pose. Behind him, thunder.

The air smelled sweet. The wind picked up.

"Holy shit," said Kayla. "I think it's going to storm."

Claire said, "I'm going inside after this."

Meanwhile, Grady took two large steps back, up the slope of the roof, and set his eyes on his target.

In a flash, he ran toward the edge, throwing himself off. Dom made it look easier, but he was also bigger. While Grady flew, Cossel held his breath.

The roar of displaced water. A dusting of mist.

Breathe out.

Grady came out of the water, his hair matted to his face, a smile spread across his lips. "Fuck dude, you gotta do it."

"No, I don't," said Cossel. "I don't gotta do shit. No fucking way."

"It's starting to rain anyways," said Erica, eyeing a droplet on her palm. "We should go inside."

Grady and Dom exchanged hand slaps. Cossel stared at the roof.

TWO

The townhouse was a sliver of home. It sat between two other homes that inexplicably felt larger than the one wedged between them. Ed Hoyer knew that couldn't be the case, because he looked up what the others went for and they listed the same square footage, and went for similar prices, adjusted for inflation. Still, when he got back home, he had to look at his feet so as not to begin sizing them up immediately.

The apron strings in his hand ran along the meager sidewalk to his front door, swaying in an erratic dance. He threw it on the table as soon as he got inside. When Vee said hello, he was already unbuttoning his shirt.

"Are the kids home?" he asked.

Vee was lying on the couch, stretching. "No," she said. "Wren is at work. Coss is at a friend's."

Ed nodded and removed his pants in response. "I'm just going to get changed."

He trudged up the stairs, nearly nude, and found a pair of sweatpants, an old T-shirt, and his laptop. He brought it down with him, trudging once again. He felt old, he suspected Vee did too, but they didn't talk about that. They weren't really old. Nearing middle age, burning through the twilight of their thirties. Still, they complained of aches and pains.

Ed sighed and fell into the couch opposite of his wife. Between them was a coffee table. He opened the laptop and let it boot.

"Do you work tomorrow?" he asked.

"At eleven."

"Are they going to get you more hours?"

"I don't know. I asked."

"Okay."

Ed watched the Windows logo on the screen.

Vee motioned to the computer. "Has anything changed?"

"I don't know, maybe."

"Can't you check it on your phone?"

"I deleted the app. Too distracting. I just check it once a day now. I think it's better this way."

Ed ground his teeth and avoided looking at his wife. The TV was on, but she wasn't watching it. She had her phone out, she was scrolling. Then, she stopped and placed the phone back down.

A large graph with a swan-diving squiggly line consumed his attention.

"Is it still going down?"

"These kinds of things rise and fall. Wax and wane, that's just how it goes." He rubbed his goatee, adjusted his glasses. Mentally, this was an act of professorial play. Ed was doing his best to be an expert, to defuse the fight before it began.

She shook her head.

On the television, an ad for the Bahamas played. A sun-kissed couple drank drinks with twisty straws on the beach. Vee sat up. "Oh look, somewhere we'll never go."

Ed looked at his computer, pretended to ignore her.

"Kylie and Joseph went to France. They actually did it. They just packed up and left, for a whole month. Can you believe that?"

"They were saving for a while." He cleared his throat. "These articles here... they suggest—"

"Jesus fucking Christ."

"They *suggest* that there might be an upturn soon."

"How much of an upturn?"

"Two or three points, maybe."

"That's nothing."

"These things take time."

"It didn't take time for us to lose."

He closed the laptop, snapping it shut. "The market is volatile. I don't know what you want from me."

Ed was never sure how these conversations started, but they always ended the same way.

Tears welled in Vee's eyes. He raised his hands, as if to repeat, *I don't know what you want from me.*

"A lot of people's portfolios are down."

"We have no savings," she said. "We have no vacations. We have two kids."

"One is about to leave."

"We have one thousand dollars in fake money. Do you remember how much we used to have, Ed?"

"You know I do."

A sob came from her throat. "Ten thousand. Gone."

The story had become something of tragic folklore between them. He'd heard it told many different times, with many different numbers. Sometimes they have saved eleven thousand, other times it was nearly twelve. Sometimes, his friend Shawn—the one who "got him into this shit"—was to blame also. Right now though, his heart sank, because he didn't have the nerve to tell Vee that their thousand dollars was now six hundred. He did his best to set the course right, to finish the story the only way he knew.

"It's not gone until we sell," said Ed. He stood up, and went to his wife, wrapping his arms around her as she struggled against him. "We bought high, it happens. It was a mistake. But long term, markets grow. That's what happens to markets. We just have to wait it out."

Vee rolled her eyes, buried her face into Ed's shoulder. He waited for her response. Usually, it was something like: *I'm just so tired of being poor.* This time though, she said, in almost a whisper, "Sometimes, I want to kill myself."

Ed stood still, a statue, and patted impotently on his wife's back.

"I don't know if I don't want to live, or just don't want to live like this," she continued.

"I don't know what to say. I don't know what to do. We're both working. We're trying, right?"

She looked him in the eyes. "If things don't get better, I'm going to do it. I don't care," she said. "I'm just so tired."

THREE

Wren thought the man looked funny, strange. But not in a way that you'd laugh at. This was the sort of fellow you'd look away from, if you could. She knew this, because she was taking his order, and as much as she wanted to look away, she couldn't.

He was not tall, maybe 5'5", and rotund—nearly jolly. Rosy cheeks popped out like strawberries in a limestone quarry. His hair was black, gelled tight down to his skull, coming together into a wicked-looking V on his forehead. He wore a black suit, with a black shirt, and black shoes. His socks were a vibrant peach.

The man ordered coffee with lots of sugar and lots of cream, alongside a cheeseburger. He called it though, specifically, "An American cheeseburger."

Wren nodded her way through this interaction as best she could, then gleefully departed into the kitchen.

Plates full of steak, eggs, and the occasional American cheeseburger made it to the pass-through where urgent hands whisked them away to hungry tables. Cory and Del had called out, Mike cursed between every plate.

"Jesus, you see that guy?"

"We get a hundred of them a night," said Mike.

I can't wait to be out of this hell hole, thought Wren, twisting her lips into a smile as she tugged on gloves and grabbed a metal spatula.

She'd only been at Cherie's for three months, but was already the only server who could also cook—a fact she liked to show off in between taking orders.

Mike said, "I'm going outside for a minute." He put two fingers to his lips, the international sign for *smoke*.

Wren nodded, organizing tickets.

Recently, Wren came to the conclusion that Springfield was one of the worst places in the world. She'd made the realization while exhaling a lungful of weed, as her friends made plans for their futures. And as the pot worked its way into her blood, her heart slammed a marathon rhythm inside her chest. One panic attack later, she was gnawing at her surroundings like a rat in a cage.

Thunder cracked and the lights flickered. "Are you fucking kidding me?"

"It's raining," said Mike.

In the dining room, customers looked up at the lights, waiting to catch them flicker.

She called through the pass-through. "No more orders. Powers gonna go out."

Blue light illuminated the dining room.

"Mike, get back in here! We need to finish these tickets or we're fucked."

She hunched over to peer through the dining room, the man in black pulled a white handkerchief and dabbed at his mouth, like someone from an old movie. *Fucking weirdo,* she thought.

"You gonna plate?"

She jumped. Mike was already back, half-burnt cig tucked behind his ear.

"Jesus, dude."

"Sorry."

He scraped the grill and sighed, outside the thunder grew louder.

Wren called back, "One chicken sandwich, one Denver omelet, and one," she paused, staring at her handwriting. "One American cheeseburger."

Cherie's contained within it a persistent hum. The refrigerators and fryers vibrated along to a sustained note, one that was so pervasive it rendered itself unrecognizable. So, when the lights went out, and the hum vanished, both Wren and the remaining customers began clearing their throats to vanquish the silence.

Most of the customers had eaten and left. The tickets were gone. The staff began to clean while they braced quietly for the inevitable.

The power down happened instantly. Distantly, there was a crash. Then, the lights turned off and the equipment ceased its hum.

Out in the lobby, Wren heard customers mumble half-hearted jokes to themselves. "Welp, guess it's closing time."

"Mike, what do we do?"

Mike shrugged. "Leave. Come back in the morning. Can't do this shit in the dark."

"Everyone hear that?" She didn't have to yell, it was quiet enough that the other servers could hear her loud and clear. Customers did too, and the ones that had not already left began to gather their things.

She went to the manager's office and pilfered her desk for a flashlight. "I'm going to help front of house, Mike. Lock the back door, please."

"Yeah, yeah."

She grabbed a stack of take-home clamshells and began to distribute them to the remaining customers, enough to count on one hand.

Across the dining room, the man in black was laughing with another server, touching her. His white fingers curled around her arm.

Fuck.

She'd been in the exact same situation as the girl who stood there now, laughing along while silently praying for someone to save her.

Wren bounded across the dining room to the man's table. "Hey, Marta. Mike needs help in the back."

Marta turned, smiling. "Oh, okay. It's just—"

"Sorry," said the man. "I didn't want to take dear Marta off task, it's only, I had asked, and thought, perchance, that she could help me, dutifully, with something on the morrow." He then raised his hands, an act of submission. "And to prove that I'm no liar, let me deliver this unto you: my flyer."

He reached into his coat and handed her a crudely copied black and white flyer. "Tomorrow," he said, waving his index finger like a ticking clock. "Don't be late."

Marta stared at the flyer and Wren cocked her head in confusion. The man in black left the booth and disappeared into the night.

FOUR

Cossel wished very much that he had not come. He did not know these people, even his friend seemed unknowable. They traded stories like they were part of a secret club. He felt himself ice over, his tongue was thick in his mouth. He couldn't do anything but continue to drink.

Grady sat next to Erica now. Dom positioned himself between Kayla and Claire, cozy on the couch. Cossel sat in an armchair across from both of them.

The lights went out.

"Knew it," said Dom.

"Fuck, I have flashlights," said Kayla.

"Do we need them?" said Grady.

Cossel imagined his friend's hand was already well up Claire's thigh.

"I like the dark," said Erica. "It's fun. Sexy."

Dom snickered. "What time are your parents home?"

"Midnight, maybe later. They're going to see some old band in the city. Probably won't be here for a while."

Everyone had hit their marks. The target was clearly set. Even in the light, Cossel was invisible, but now he also felt trapped. *There's no way Grady's going to want to leave now.* He considered his options and began the early drafting of an excuse.

"We could play a game. Like twenty questions, or never have I ever," said Kayla.

"Ooh, that could be fun," said Claire.

An optimistic part of him bloomed. He understood games. He liked games. He could be a part of a game. "Sure," he said, with rubbery lips.

"I have a good one," said Dom. "A really good one."

Cossel shifted uncomfortably.

"Spill."

"It's called Raise the Dead."

"How do you play?" asked Grady.

"Easy. In this game, each of us is dead. But one of us is a necromancer."

"What's that?" asked Cossel.

"That is someone who can raise the dead. The goal of the game is to stay dead. If we're touched by the necromancer, we live. But that's the fun part. You see, the dead tell no tales, so those living can discuss and share information. You win when it's down to two people, and the living have to guess who's dead and who's a necromancer."

"Oh, I get it. It's sorta like Werewolf," said Kayla.

"Exactly."

"So, whoever the necromancer is has to be super sneaky."

"Correct. And the dead can't talk."

Cossel writhed in his seat. "So, how do we decide who is who?"

"A simple drawing will suffice," said Dom. "Kayla, do we have a room that we can play this in, where the moonlight won't let us see who's who?"

"The basement."

"Perfect."

Before long, there were six tears of paper, each with a scribbled role on it. "Okay," he said. "Come forward. Remember, don't tell anyone your role."

All of the torn bits of paper were dropped into a small bowl. Claire went up first, pocketing her paper after reading it by moonlight. Then it was Dom, Erica, and Grady. Cossel approached the bowl with casual recklessness—he felt as if he were driving head-on into traffic. Rain fell hard outside, a liquid pitter-patter, that combined with his buzz, made him feel almost cozy. He slid the piece of paper around the porcelain of the small bowl, dragging it up the lip to pinch between his fingers. He unfolded it. In hastily scrawled lettering was the word: *necromancer.*

He pocketed the note and went back to the group, secretly ecstatic at the changing of tides.

Under the white light of their phone screens, they traveled one by one into the basement. "Find a place and stay in it, you're dead," said Dom.

They each found their place in the absolute darkness, only the faintest of light touched them—a silvery echo of moonlight that reflected off dewy glass behind rectangular windows.

"Okay, this is it," said Dom. "The game's starting. No more talking, unless you were resurrected."

Cossel couldn't see anything but could hear faint rustlings.

He moved into the center of the room, slowly army-crawling. Cossel's heart thumped in his chest. He was fully committed to winning.

Five minutes passed and he had not moved. He staved off boredom by imagining the others' surprised faces when it was he who became the victor. Another five minutes had passed in silence, and he wondered what sort of game this was. How could anyone find anyone in this blackness? How could they have any idea who it was? Who amongst them was left? He thought on this for a moment, and suddenly, an idea sprang to mind.

He stood, not bothering to hide the sounds of his body. He sighed and said, "Alright, looks like I'm out."

Cossel felt for the door, inching himself to the edge of the room. Quietly, he smiled. He felt devious, like a wolf amongst sheep.

A flash of sheet lightning. His eyes searched frantically. *One, two, three, four…*

He caught all of them, in a glimpse. And then he glanced down, as the burst of light flickered, and he saw Dom beside his feet, looking up at him with glassy expectant eyes.

Cossel's heart stuttered.

When the room was black, he used the sound of thunder to mask his movements, carefully walking to where Erica sat, her knees up against her chest. He kneeled, then tapped her shoe.

"Fuck," she said.

A couple long strides back. "What? Who's that?"

"Erica," she said. "I got got."

"I'm just glad I have someone else to talk to now."

"Fuck. Yeah, this shit was getting boring."

Cossel felt strange having a conversation when there were so many people in the room, staring into the darkness, looking for them.

"Do you know who touched you?" he asked, laboriously uninterested.

"No, they touched my shoe. You?"

"They got me on the arm. I thought it was you, honestly. Or one of the other girls."

"Kayla? Erica?" She called. "You hear that? We're on to you."

"I guess we just have to wait now?"

"That's all this game is. Waiting."

Cossel found his place next to Dom again, quietly.

He knew Grady was directly across the room from him. He was emboldened now. He planted the seed. All he had to do was leave Kayla and Claire alone, and either way, he won.

He struck Grady's pant leg with a playful stroke, meant to be light and tentative.

"I'm out," said Grady. "Someone touched my pant leg."

Erica said, "Yay! Welcome to the world of the living! Follow my voice."

Amidst the shuffling, Cossel fumbled in the dark to tag Dom.

"Alright, guys. I'm here too," said Dom.

"Welcome, welcome," said Cossel.

"It's been a party."

"This game is fucking boring, dude," said Erica.

"Well, this is where it gets interesting though."

"Show us."

"Kayla and Claire are our two remainders. Right? They can't answer, but process of elimination."

Grady said, "My money's on Kayla."

"I'll vote for that, just to get it done with," said Erica.

"I'll third Kayla. 50-50 shot, right?" added Cossel, deviously unassuming.

"You're all too hasty," said Dom, and suddenly Cossel felt sick. "Remember that the necromancer can speak at any time. Any one of us can be the necromancer as well."

"That does make it more interesting," said Erica.

"Indeed it does," said Cossel weakly.

"If we're still open to another guess, let's think of one of the more obvious strategies of this game. If you were a necromancer, and wanted to fool us, what would you do?"

"You'd pretend to be gotten, take yourself out of the suspect pool," said Grady.

"Ooh, clever."

"Exactly," said Dom. "Except it's not that clever because everyone thinks of it."

Cossel bit the inside of his cheeks.

"So, who's your guess?" asked Erica.

"Cossel," said Dom. "He was the first one out, and I don't know about you guys, but I didn't hear anything. No rustling, no nothing. No one is completely silent, right? I called it from the start, honestly."

"No way, man," said Cossel.

"But that's exactly what the necromancer would say," said Erica.

"I could see it," said Grady. "Coss is a shitty liar. He always sounds like he's hiding something. I'm changing my vote." Boyish cruelty sharpened every consonant.

"What happens if you all vote for me and I'm not the necromancer?"

"We're out then, we lost. You choose your pick, and the necromancer reveals themself."

"Fine," he said. "Do what you will."

"I see what you're saying," said Erica. "He does have something about him. Like he seems like he's trying too hard to be normal. If you know what I mean?"

"Does that mean you're changing your vote?"

"Yep," said Erica. "I'm all aboard the 'Cossel is a necromancer' train."

"The tribe has spoken. Cossel?"

In the blackness of the room, he shook his head. Puberty was such that sometimes boys cried when they did not want to. He swallowed a sob like a chunk of prime beef and said, too gregariously. "Yep, you got me."

"Too easy," said Dom. "Guess that means you lose."

Kayla gasped. "Finally."

"Thank god that shit is over."

Then, the lights turned on and Cossel covered his eyes. "Jesus, it's fucking bright…"

Grady had his arm around Erica as she whispered in his ear. Claire and Kayla had their phones out, studying their missed messages. Meanwhile, Dom stared at Cossel, still and cat-like.

"It's just a fucking game," he said, finally.

Cossel blinked away the wetness that ringed his eyes, unsure of why his loss hurt at all.

Claire looked up from her phone. "I gotta go, guys. Mom's coming to get me."

"You will be missed," said Dom.

They filtered back into the living room and the weight on Cossel's heart only grew heavier. He developed an anxiety he never knew he had. New insecurities blossomed inside of him, germinating new fears.

When Claire left, Erica pulled Kayal aside. After a moment of conspiratorial whispering, Erica announced that she was going to go upstairs and asked if Grady would go with her.

He jumped at the chance, his arm twisting serpentine around her waist.

"Use protection," said Dom.

Cossel laughed along with the rest of them.

Then, when it was just the three of them, the conversation seemed to dip and dart away from Cossel. Really, it was Dom and Kayla talking. Dom and Kayla on the couch, touching and laughing. Then, whispering. Then, looking his way and laughing again.

Cossel sat, trapped inside of himself.

"We're going to retire, dear necromancer," said Dom.

They got up, giggling, Kayla said, "Feel free to help yourself… to whatever."

"No, no," he said, standing. "I've got to get going."

"Okay," she said, but she wasn't looking at him, she was resting her head in Dom's arm. "Thanks for coming."

And then they were gone.

He swallowed again. He thought about what his dad would say, how he'd regale him with stories from the supermarket. *One time, this big motherfucker got in my face and told me he'd kill me if I didn't take a coupon.* He always told the stories like they were funny. Maybe that was the ticket to making this one sting less too. Maybe he had to make it funny. He tried.

One time, I tried to impress a lot of people I didn't like, and I ended up looking like a clown. Honk honk, wanna balloon?

Alone, he walked around the first floor of the house. It was bright, marvelous. Larger than his own home many times over. The bathroom had a jacuzzi hot tub. The oven was topped with a large industrial brushed metal hood. The fridge dispensed water and ice—perhaps the surest sign of relative wealth there ever was.

He tried not to think about his evening, but it was a fruitless effort. His cheeks burned red and his humiliation transformed into anger. Cossel balled his fists in Kayla's kitchen and imagined her look of horror after hypothetically punching a fist through her wall. Dom's chides echoed in his brain, hitting him again and again in the same sore spots. Cossel gritted his teeth and blinked away a new flush of tears.

He wiped them away. *I need to get home*, he thought. *I need to get out of here.*

Cossel left the lovely living room with the tall ceilings and many windows. The storm had left its remnants scattered all across the pool. Dead leaves and earth muddied the once blue water. Cossel chuckled at this small justice.

He was about to leave, seconds away from pushing past the hinged door and onto the street, when he turned back—a nagging thought pulling at his brain folds. *No, I can't.*

But looking at the ladder, he thought he could.

His eyes followed each grooved step, all the way up to the roof. It leaned in front of a window. For a moment, he considered peering in, watching Grady or Dom fumble their way through teenaged sex while he snickered. But his eyeline moved to the roof.

I think I can make it, he thought.

He bobbed in place, adrenaline rushing through his veins. This new energy was the direct result of transubstantiation, he had transformed sadness to anger and now to boyish risk-taking. Cossel placed a hand on the ladder, testing its cold metallic grip in his hands. Then, carefully, he placed a foot on it.

Smothering his thoughts, he climbed, pausing for only a fruitless second at the window.

On the roof, he steadied himself on all fours, then stood tall and mighty under the moonlight. Warm booze kept him loose and thoughtless. He meandered for only a second, before finding his perch along the roof's edge. "A long way down," he said, exorcizing an intrusive thought.

The pool no longer shimmered. It was an ugly thing. Branches floated in it, dust swirled, leaves clumped together in cysts along its still surface. It was further away than it looked. *Maybe I was right the first time?* he thought.

Cossel shook his head. *Nope.* He refused to think. His body was a machine now. It took four steps back, up the sloping roof. It made him crouch low, with his weight on his back foot, and when he started toward the lip, he sprang—one foot in front of the other as he made his way to the edge and leapt.

Only, the roof was wet.

It only took one weak shingle.

Right as his foot began to lift off, as he threatened to float to space, the shingle came loose and he slipped—just a couple inches. The top of him did that thing that cartoon characters do. His arms were windmills, he opened his mouth wide and said, "Oh woah woah." On tiptoes, he fell forward. Not up and out. But forward, face down, a belly flop toward concrete.

In the air, he adjusted, slightly. His feet went under him, like a cannonball. He straightened out. Somehow, he'd done a whole front flip. For a brief moment, he saw the water and thought that he'd feel it, that it'd break his fall and everything would turn out okay. It was a 50-50 shot, he figured. There was him—the amazing floating boy; then there was the pool lip. Unforgiving concrete on one side, soft safe chlorinated water on the other.

Right before his feet buckled before him, he was sure everything would turn out right.

But then the pain shot up through his legs.

He tried to course correct, leaning forward, to try to get into the water. But his ankle collapsed under his weight. He was leaning forward on the side of his foot, smashed into the poolside at a 90-degree angle. And for whatever reason, it didn't give, not like he thought it would, because then his knee went *backwards*.

When the water hit, he was in shock. His lungs filled with water and he screamed at the same time. Drowning and screaming. Flailing. His leg was numb to the touch. His knee was loose and screaming. He tried to kick it, but he couldn't get his foot to work right. *Fuck*, he thought. *Fuck fuck fuck.*

The pool wasn't deep. The black paint on the side marked it for six feet. But Cossel wasn't tall. It was plenty to drown in. He imagined his friends would find him, standing straight up, pale like a fish's belly, with a mere four inches of water above his head.

Cossel used his good leg—or rather, his better leg—to leap up and down, frantically; expelling mouthfuls of water and taking in deep lungfuls of air. His fingers grasped the side of the pool, his heart beat in his ears, he lifted himself.

The pain was incredible.

As he hauled himself out of the pool, his dangling leg screamed in a pain he'd never dared to imagine. Nerves went off like atom bombs. He rolled over on the concrete and let out a sputtering breath.

Cossel didn't hear the sliding door open.

FIVE

Wren's phone buzzed in her pocket. One, two, three, four times. Home wasn't far, but she always drove. Springfield was a normal town, but it is normal for women to be robbed, raped, and killed. Wren was careful in that regard.

The phone stopped and started buzzing again. Wren ground her teeth. She bit down harder when she saw it was her brother. Cossel liked to call her. He'd made it a habit to call her instead of Mom or Dad. It was like a switch went off when she turned eighteen. She was suddenly an adult, and because she was a *young* adult, she was perceived as safe.

The road was wet. She drove carefully around branches and other debris. Cossel's name kept flashing.

She didn't mind it, some of the time. Other times, it made her feel that much more like a caged animal. When Wren closed her eyes, she felt the rest of her life hurtling toward her. It was unimaginably heavy, and unimaginably fast. Every possible experience from now till her death threatened to crush her, to push the air out of her lungs. It was both exhilarating and terrifying. Sometimes, she was in control and the future was definable. Other times, she was being pulled by hooks back into the maudlin present.

Drunk? Was he drunk? No, Cossel doesn't drink. Maybe he does. I don't know. I didn't. Well, just a little.

The phone went silent, the blinking stopped, just as she arrived home. *Three more months,* she thought, staring at their

32

slender home. In the quiet of the driveway, she laid her head on the steering wheel and breathed deeply. The silence after the storm was a beautiful, quiet taste of death.

When she raised her head from the steering wheel, the peace was gone.

Her father slammed the door, her mother was on the phone. They hustled into the family car, their faces white.

"Are you coming?" he asked, fumbling for his keys.

Extreme pain changes the way you think. It precisely excises all the bullshit and leaves you with your authentic self. There is no pretense in extreme pain. There is yelling, crying, screaming, cursing, blubbering, aching, begging—but no pretense.

When they picked him up, he didn't care what look Dom wore on his face. His desires were distilled and diluted. The thought of a new car—a shit heap—vanished from his mind. Before, that was his only true desire. Now, being carefully lifted by his father, no longer too proud to cry, no longer scared to curse, the only thing he wanted was the pain to stop.

He was barely aware that there wasn't enough room in the car.

Wren's voice, sharply saying, "Why the fuck am I even here?" floated past him. He knew, vaguely, that she was there upon arrival. But he couldn't track the conversation well enough to know where she ended up. On the ride to the ER, he was alone in the backseat, stretched out. His leg swole up to fill his pant leg. He couldn't move his ankle, let alone his toes. Cossel's breaths ran ragged but that's all he thought about. He didn't hear a word of his parent's chatter.

Wren stood out in front of the street, phone to ear. "Pick up, pick up, pick up," she pleaded.

"Hey! This is Tracy, leave a message—"

She ended the call.

Her arms wrapped tight around her midsection. Fourteen phone calls and no answers. She might have stomped if she was sure no one was looking, but she was all too aware of Cossel's friends hanging out at the pool, piecing together whatever-the-fuck happened.

I would've taken my own car if—

"Hey, do you need a ride?"

A young boy, maybe sixteen or seventeen, cupped his hands around his mouth. He had dark curly hair and the arrogant smile of someone who knew they were handsome. He pointed at her, like she might not know who he was yelling at.

Before Wren could say anything, before she could think it through, he held a hand up. "Wait a minute," he said. "I can take you home. Let me get my keys."

She stammered. "Okay—sure—I was just calling for a ride—"

But the boy had already disappeared into the house.

He's a kid, she thought. *He's probably safe.*

Probably.

Wren held her arms closer to herself, protective. When he came back out, he was smiling. She loosened her grip. It felt wrong to think poorly of someone smiling.

They didn't get to him right away. They never do.

People get hurt in storms. People have heart attacks. That's just the nature of the beast. They didn't care that a sixteen-year-old boy couldn't think. They didn't care that he'd never broken anything before. He'd have to wait.

Cossel let his mother run her fingers through his hair and tried to think of nothing.

Wren said, "So, is this yours?" The question came after a gentle stall in the conversation. After she questioned him about her brother, after he asked her why she was standing in the middle of the road, looking mad. When the answers came, or lack thereof, she found herself wondering about the boy himself, his car.

The boy, Dom, said, "It is." A knowing smile crossed his lips that Wren couldn't help but find endearing. "Real rich kid shit, I know."

"At least you're honest."

"Well, that's to say—I understand how this looks. But it's not how it looks."

"How does it look?"

"Like daddy bought me something nice and I'm flaunting."

"So, what is it really?"

He grinned, swerving smoothly around a fallen branch. "I *earned* this."

"How?" It was a question, but it was an automatic one—perfunctory. Wren didn't truly care, but she did want to keep this eerily confident young man talking. There was something electric about him.

"I've got a side hustle. Just a little thing. Helping with a firm that just came to town."

"Like a law firm?"

"No, marketing. Research. Consumer personas and stuff like that."

"How do you help with that?"

Here, for the first time, Dom faltered. His good-natured demeanor shifted, and Wren saw a glimpse of a confused boy underneath. "I just do what they tell me, I guess. They're hiring, you know?"

"Yeah. Come by sometime."

The car slowed to a stop in front of her house. "Thanks for the lift," she said.

"No problem." Dom twisted in his seat. "Hey, take this."

"What is it?"

She grabbed a folded piece of paper from his hands.

"A flyer," he said. "For that thing."

A cold chill crept down her back.

Dom drove off into the night and Wren stared at the battered flyer. She scanned the top line again and again. *From the offices of Cormorant/Carmichael.*

SIX

The room was not a room, but a series of powder blue curtains arranged in a square. Cossel laid on a cot, his leg elevated, drugged blissfully out of his mind. Three adults stood around him, meticulously examining plastic cards while he drifted along on a warm, dreamless current.

"This is all current?" asked the nurse.

"I don't know. I think so. They send them out every two years. It's probably current." Ed shrugged. "That's what they gave me."

The nurse frowned, but said nothing further.

Vee said, "When will we see the X-rays?"

"I don't know. The doctor will be here soon."

When the nurse left, questions roiled within them.

Vee paced back and forth. "What was he doing? Do you think he wanted to…?"

"No," said Ed, shaking his head. "I doubt it. He's a happy boy. A good kid."

"Did you see the way the doctor looked at him?"

"They haven't said anything yet."

She snorted. "Of course they haven't said anything yet. Because it's *bad*. They usually try to reassure you, right?"

Ed sat back. He threw his hands up. With his small frame, he looked something like a scarecrow. "We don't know anything yet."

37

Both of them stared at the IV stuck in their son's arm, and both of them, for a brief moment, wondered how much a bag of the stuff costs.

Cossel turned slightly, his mouth hung open as if he were going to say something. He smacked his lips, drool coming from the corners of his mouth, then shook his head slightly, as if to say "Aw, fuck it," then went back to sleep. The whole time, Ed wondered if that's how it'd be for the rest of his life. He shivered.

In another ten minutes, the doctor came. "Evening, folks. This Cossel, here? Where's that name come from, anyway?" His smile eased them.

"Nowhere," said Vee. "We made it up. My parents gave me a made-up name too. My name is Vee, but it doesn't stand for anything."

"Cossel." The doctor let the name sit on his tongue. "I like it. Cossel, can you hear me?"

Cossel took a deep, dreamy breath. "Yes," he said.

"That's good. Alright, you probably feel a little loopy right now. We got you on a good cocktail to numb the pain a bit. The good news is you didn't break anything."

"Thank god," said Ed.

"The bad news though is that this is quite a serious injury." On the word serious, the doctor's face melted from smile to frown. "You've severed several vital ligaments, most importantly your ACL. You know what the ACL is? You ever watch football?"

Cossel shook his head like it was underwater.

"The ACL is an important ligament that keeps your knee in place. Sports players sometimes tear theirs and have to sit out a season. That's why I was asking if you watch football—it happens to a lot of football players. Soccer too. Which is also football. Funny. The other thing is that you sorta squashed your peroneal nerve. That's why you can't move your foot." He then scraped his fingernails down the side of Cossel's legs. "Do you feel that?"

"No," he said.

"Alright, yeah. So you've lost feeling in your leg. It might come back, it might not. You can't lift your foot, can you?"

"No."

"That's drop foot. It's more common than you think. You'll have to be careful walking. Be very careful, or you might take a spill and things can get worse."

Vee reached out, squeezed her son's hand. "How long will it last?"

"It could go away on its own, the nerve damage that is. There's no surgery we can do for that. There's a thirty percent chance it can heal on its own. Sometimes it does."

"And if it doesn't?" asked Ed.

"We can do surgery on his ACL and tighten that knee right back up. I'd recommend it, in fact. For the drop foot, it's a bit trickier. We could remove and replace a tendon so that he can lift his foot again, but there are no guarantees. This is, unfortunately, what we call a life-changing injury."

"Life-changing," repeated Ed.

"What does that mean? He's fucked?" said Vee.

The doctor, trained in patience, smiled like a living statue. "It means that there will likely be long-term damage. This could be some minor pain, it could be a disability that is corrected with orthotics, or with surgery, it might be nothing at all."

Cossel, slurring, said, "I want the surgery."

"Surgery. How much does the surgery cost?"

The doctor grimaced. "I can't say for sure. It depends on the insurance. Out of pocket, it'd likely cost ten thousand. That's a rough estimate."

Ed shifted in his seat, avoiding Vee's gaze.

"For now, Cossel, we're giving you a brace, crutches, and some medication. Just for a week or two. Stay positive, buddy.

This isn't a death sentence. It's life-changing, not life-ending."

Ed and Vee watched their son, who drifted off to sleep, drugged and oblivious. Ed's hand reached for Vee's, but she refused to grasp his. An inarticulate weight fell on his shoulders.

To break the silence, he chuckled in a wounded way. "God," he said, real dread creeping into his voice. "I can't wait to see the bill."

Wren ran. Down an empty suburban street—Springfield or anywhere—black and shiny from the rain. Boots slapped the ground behind her, coupled with the grunts and groans of their owners. She turned back, hot air burning her tongue, to see a small crowd of people—normal people—with white eyes and cracked pupils that swirled in a spiral out to the edges of their eyes. *Cartoon hypnotist eyes*, she thought.

They ran after her with torches. She didn't know why they had torches. No one carries torches anymore. The orange firelight lit their faces, emphasizing the black in their shadows.

She ran harder and faster. *I can't keep going. They're going to catch me.*

They were gaining on her, the footsteps were getting closer. They weren't going to stop.

"Why are you chasing me? Why are you doing this to me?"

Up ahead, she spotted something. She jogged harder. There it was, safety. An ornate building, all columns and spires. An amalgam of Gothic and classical architecture. She thought it looked like something she saw in a book once. Maybe a storybook. The swirly-eyed people behind her were gaining though, and she knew that all the neighborhood doors were locked. Obviously, no one was going to save her because her neighbors were all behind her. They were carrying torches.

This strange monument—Wren did not know why she called it that—was her only chance.

She ran up its steps, into the black folds of darkness between its columns. For a brief moment, Wren spun around to see the townspeople and their wild-eyed procession. Their teeth gnashed. Violence pumped through their veins.

Wren hid in the dark and listened for their footsteps.

PRODUCT

SEVEN

In the middle of the night, Cossel got up to take a piss. His leg was still swollen, moving it made him feel like he was fighting against a downed tree. He joked in front of others that it was the leg of a taller man. He did a lot of joking in the week after his accident. But alone in the dark, while his family slept, he eyed the distance from his bed to his crutches with dread.

Cossel could stand, barely. He lifted himself off his bed, using his arms for support. From the bed, he transferred his hands to his nightstand. From the nightstand, he found a windowsill. He stepped carefully, lifting his left leg higher than the right. It hurt to do so, bending at the knee made everything worse, but he'd already had two near-slips in the last day, and the darkness provoked caution. With some effort, he made it to his crutches, situated them under his armpits, and swung himself slowly to the bathroom, where he took his piss and went back to his room.

There was no one to joke with back in his bed. He replayed the phone call to Grady in his mind. *God, you fucked yourself up bad.*

A little too much to drink.

I'll say.

And that's all it became in his own private mythos: a drunken tale of debauchery. *Wanna know how I got this scar, kid?*

The conversation with Grady went well, the way most conversations with teenage boys go—dodging vulnerability in favor of in-jokes and absurd proclamations. But as Cossel replayed it, there was one statement that stuck in his mind.

So, you're pretty much a cripple now? Forever?

Whenever he thought of that and the plain way Grady said it, it made him want to vomit. Despite what the doctor said, *forever* had not sunk in. There was no forever for teenagers. There was today and tomorrow.

No, I just need surgery, he said. *Then I'll be fine.*

The power of those words was what kept him going. When he texted his friends, it was as good as a salutation. *Hey man, can't go anywhere for a while. At least, until I get surgery.*

Drunk story to surgery story was a good, strong pipeline.

He hobbled over to his bed, leaning his crutches against the wall. He twisted toward the bed and pain shot through his knee. The night was cool and still. He popped an oxy and settled into bed. Slowly, carefully.

Ed typed his employee ID number into the machine. He still had to clock on, despite technically being a part of the management team. The soft roar of the store screamed behind him. He tied the apron behind his back, scratched at his goatee, and embraced a busy grocery store on the first of the month.

It was Saturday. EBT benefits had arrived. They would have trouble keeping the shelves stocked, he knew.

Underneath the fluorescent lights, customers tapped their toes in line at the check stands. He tapped a cart gently, and said his line, "I can getcha right over here." It was friendly, disarming, and infinitely practiced. Five customers later, he was in a daze, zoning out. When this happened, he almost always imagined his own future wealth. He pictured himself in a large house with vast amenities. Most important to this fantasy was what he wore and what he did. In his imagination, he always wore a nice suit—the sort of thing James Bond would wear. The legs of the trousers were cropped, shorter than he was accustomed to. He saw the young people in Springfield wear pants like that, proudly showing their argyle socks. Distantly, he acknowledged he had the means to do the same thing, but he also had the feeling that he was not the type of person to do that. Some people could pull it off, some couldn't. The assistant manager at the regional grocery store chain could not. Taste and expression were always something to be cultivated amidst wealth. As he was now, his clothes were ill-fitting, occasionally stained. Function, over fashion.

In this fantasy, he wore fine clothes with stylistic embellishments. And what he did in those clothes was nothing. He did nothing, or at least not anything he didn't want to. It was a special sort of leisure.

Ed typed produce codes automatically, miles away in a better life until the phone rang at his check stand, forcing him back to earth. "Excuse me," he said to the elderly gentleman in front of him.

On the phone: "We're having a meeting."

"Right, I know," he said. "We're busy though."

"Close up. We need you there."

"Okay," he said. He handed a closed sign to the man, who didn't seem to know what to do with it. "Just… go ahead and put it on the end. Yes, just like that."

Five minutes later, he was climbing a narrow flight of concrete stairs to a small break room, bullpen, and a conference room. He set his face in stone and kept repeating words about Stoicism he read on social media.

The room was filled with four other bored aprons. Two men, two women. In the center of them was Kyle.

Kyle was tall, slender, with spiked and thinning red-blond hair. His smiles always made his eyes squint so much that they looked like black pebbles embedded beneath his faint eyebrows. "There he is," he said.

"I'm here," he said. "I made it." Ed took a seat, unfolding a plastic chair. "What's on the docket today?"

"Hiring," said Kyle. "We're talking about hiring."

One of the other aprons said, "Julia quit, so did Fred."

"I just put in my two weeks," said a bespectacled apron named Shawn. "I'll be gone too."

A pang of disappointment hit Ed unexpectedly. He liked Shawn. "Sorry to hear that," he said.

"Dropping like flies," said Kyle. "I wanted to discuss how we can make this a better workplace, a better…"

Ed glazed over. He went back to his fantasy house, wearing his fantasy clothes.

"Ed?"

"Yes?"

"Were you listening?"

He bit his cheek. "Sorry, I was thinking about our new till policy. What was that?"

"What do you think we can do to better serve an increase in employee retention?"

Without thinking, he said, "More money, I guess."

The other aprons nodded.

Shawn said, "I got offered three bucks more an hour at—"

The words shook Ed. "Three bucks more? That's more than I make."

"They're hiring, baby."

Kyle put his hands up. "Obviously, we don't have the budget to give everyone a three dollar an hour raise. But what if we threw a pizza party? Say, every quarter?"

Ed nodded, his eyes threatening to close under the weight of last night's ER visit.

A chorus of "Sure, sounds good," sang with hoarse, tired voices.

"It's something, right?"

Ed said, "I think it's a good call," he said. "Show people they're appreciated." His voice came out monotone, zombie-like. So much so that the rest of the management team, everyone but Kyle, laughed.

"We don't have the budget for anything else," said Kyle.

Shawn shook his head. "Then, why are you having this meeting?"

"You don't need to be here, you can leave."

"You wanted opinions and you got opinions. The money fucking sucks here, dude."

Ed couldn't help but smile at the kid's boldness, but he was already on thin ice. "Why don't you help out on the floor, Shawn. You're not gonna be here in two weeks anyway."

Shawn shrugged. "Alright, fine." He got up without protest. Ed figured the kid was thankful for the redirection.

"Congrats on the new job, by the way," added Ed.

"Yeah, yeah."

When Shawn left, they talked more about the same things. Ed tried to keep his place in the conversation, even as he drifted in and out of sentences. Just to be safe, he asked a question every so often. "How should we implement that?" "Who's the point person for that?" That seemed to do enough to keep him in Kyle's good graces.

He didn't mind losing people too much, because he knew Kyle hated him for some reason he could never know. And he knew that the more people quit, the more Kyle was stuck with him. Ed figured that if he was miserable, as manager, Kyle should follow suit.

The meeting adjourned with nothing gained beyond a date for a staff pizza party. They filed out of the white conference room. The rhythmic beeping of check stands filled the air. Even from their meager office, there was no escape.

Kyle tapped Ed on the shoulder. "Just a word, real quick," he said.

Ed kept his face tight, stoic like the videos said. He nodded and followed him into the office.

"What can I help you with?"

Kyle ran his hands through his thinning hair. Exasperated, he said, "I don't know what to say. Ed, this is your third strike."

"What were one and two?"

"They're in your files if you want to see them. I'm not seeing what I need to see from you here."

Rage boiled within Ed's stomach. "Are you kidding me?"

"You're insubordinate, rude. The leads talk about you like you're an anchor."

"What do they say?"

"That you're slow, that you make more work for them."

"I help them. But it's not my job to help them. I have a thousand other things to do too."

"They say that you're a weak link."

"So, you're firing me?"

"No, I'm putting you on probation." Kyle's face softened. He gestured to the chair. "Look, man. I'm not gonna pretend that we're buddies, but we should be able to work together. I feel like you're not giving me all you can. Are you looking for another job?"

"Not yet," said Ed, taking a seat.

"Well, don't. I know you think I hate you—that's the other thing people say about you, that you got a chip on your shoulder about me."

Ed's face burned with humiliation.

"But I don't hate you, Ed. I want you here. You're a good guy. I just need you to step up."

Remember the videos.

"Thank you for letting me know," said Ed. "I'm glad you felt comfortable enough with me to tell me this. I promise to show improvement."

Kyle shook his head. "The robot routine again, huh?"

"What do you want me to say?"

"I don't know, man. Just… try to give a fuck."

Outside, Ed leaned on the building. Night had come. In the parking lot, two teenagers, about the age of his son, practiced kick flips under orange streetlights. He lit a cigarette and swallowed the memory of a lost future.

He had spent most of the day replaying the conversation in his head. Sometimes he'd edit it on the fly, rewrite the script.

"I just need you to step up."

"I just need you to go fuck yourself."

But this routine only served to make him feel more anxious, more trapped.

One of the kids landed the trick, and the dry roar of wheels on asphalt became a celebration. Ed thought of telling them to be careful, that he had a kid at home with a fucked leg because he did something stupid.

But then Shawn came out of the building, earbuds stuck so deep into his ears they might as well have been touching his brain.

Ed waved at the kid, who was a full fifteen years younger, but his most treasured colleague all the same.

Shawn released one of his earbuds. "Whatcha doing out here?"

"Smoking, want one?"

The kid took a smoke from his pack. "Didn't know you smoked."

"Occasionally. Just to look cool."

Shawn laughed, lighting his cigarette with an eerily practiced hand. "You get reamed today?"

"Every day," said Ed. Even he knew he sounded pathetic. Another kickflip crashed through the parking lot, the sound of hard plastic wheels hitting pavement. Ed changed the subject. "So, where are you going off to?"

"New business. A pop-up. A consulting firm."

"Don't you need a degree for that?" Ed didn't know what a consulting firm was, but it sounded like something that *he* would never be able to do.

"Hey man, I got an associate's in business. But they're doing a lot of hiring, for all positions. Office work, focus groups, whatever."

"Yeah? And they pay good?"

"Better than here."

Ed sucked on his cigarette. "How about that?"

Shawn flicked his ash and reached toward his pocket. He pulled out his phone. "You been surviving the bear market?"

"Barely. I'm getting scared."

"Dude. Zoom out. The graphs don't lie. We're gonna be millionaires. You know what happens when you sell, don't you?"

"You lose."

"That's fucking right," said Shawn. "So, don't lose. Keep hold of it. Watch the market turn back up. If anything, buy more."

"Buy more."

"It's low right now, man. But given enough time all markets turn up. I've been pumping every cent into my portfolio, man."

"Any new coins, you've been eyeing? A Doge or a Shiba, or a—"

Shawn grinned. "Oh dude, I'll send you a list."

"My wife's gonna kill me."

"Nah, nah. She'll be thanking you in like a couple years, man. This shit is about to go off. Trust me, bro."

They discussed what cars they'd buy, what houses they'd buy, where they'd live, and how much they'd spend a day as the uber rich. Then, Shawn finished his cigarette and went off into the night. But the conversation didn't end there. Ed kept cycling within it for the rest of the night. After he clocked out, after he hugged his wife, and checked in on Cossel, after Wren swallowed back her disgust at his very existence. At night, in bed, he thought about lines on a graph—jumping steadily through time.

EIGHT

Vee brushed her hair, dark and bushy, in the mirror. She looked at her own face with a sort of growing dismay.

"Cossel, are you alright?" she yelled through the wall.

"Fine, Mom."

"Let me know if you need anything."

The walls were thin enough that they did not need to yell to reach each other.

"I have to work today at three, are you going to be okay? Dad's not gonna be home till late."

"I'll be fine," groaned her son.

She put the brush down, straightened her collar, and walked over to the next room. Cossel was laying down, he was on his phone. "How's the leg?"

"Sucks."

She nodded. "You able to move that foot yet?"

"Nope, totally dead."

Vee was pretty sure that he was trying to demonstrate, but there was no movement.

"That does suck," she said.

Cossel didn't look up from his phone. "When can we talk to the doctors about surgery?"

"I don't know. Soon, hopefully. We can make an appointment."

"I don't want to be like this forever."

"I know. I wouldn't either. Does it hurt?"

"Only when I stand on it."

"I saw you getting around without the crutches yesterday. Just a cane. That's an improvement."

Cossel looked up at her with watery eyes. His lips pursed, like he was about to say something, then didn't. Vee rubbed her hands through his hair.

"I know what it's like to be sad," she said. "They say exercise helps. Talking to people helps too."

"I can't exercise."

"But you can talk."

Cossel sighed. "Yeah. Thanks."

There was a burdensome silence between them that Vee wished to fill with everything she ever felt and had swallowed down. But instead, she remained silent. She held her son's hand. "I've got to go soon, are you sure you're going to be okay?"

"Yeah," he said.

"Okay, okay."

Vee left Cossel to himself, finished her work clothes with a scarf and coat. On the drive to work, she tried to think of nothing.

There was a crowd gathered in the parking lot. Men and women stood together, regular people, and they had their hands in their pockets or a wry smile on their lips. *They aren't holding signs*, she thought. As she parked, she considered the fact that they might be protesting something. But there were only ten of them. She unlocked the car door and stood outside, hoping to gain some idea of what was happening.

On the way into the craft store that she hated, she saw the man they stood around. He wore a black suit with a black bolo tie. His hair was slicked back, tight to his skull. He was pale and plump with a beak-like nose and red lips. It looked as if he was preaching, or rather, it looked that way because people were surrounding him, listening.

She overheard him say, "The call of money is a scream, not a whisper. Let tinnitus unite us in this. We can be eager and strong, beleaguered and wrong, but there's no sense in waiting another moment. We are beings full of doomful portent. Of important thoughts caught in decay and rot. But the answer is not: want not. It is to want all."

Vee stood in the parking lot, confused. The man was strange looking, unlike any she had ever seen. His lyrical language made no sense, yet enraptured her.

The automatic doors opened, and a blast of warm air made her cheeks flush. Paul was building a small display, the first touch of too-early Christmas to grace the store.

"Who is that man out there?"

"No idea. He's been there for hours though. My husband saw him yesterday at the mall, same spiel."

"What was he saying?"

"Fuck if I know," said Paul, hanging a reindeer above a wreath. "What's he saying now?"

Vee shrugged. "Fuck if I know."

"He's been out there for hours though. Hard not to watch. He's a talker."

"Yeah, he is," said Vee.

"How's Cossel?"

"Not great, but okay." She was still staring out the front doors, to the small crowd of people. A younger boy—about Cossel's age—circled to the members of the crowd with a ream of papers. She searched her memory. The boy with the curly black hair wore a shiny black coat. Finally, she said, "I know that boy."

Paul followed her gaze. "Oh look, it's Stacy's Mom."

"No, not like that," she said. "He's one of my son's friends, I think. He was there the night we took him to the hospital. Wren said he gave her a ride home."

"Just home?"

Vee snickered, even though she hated to think of her kids having sex. "He's a bit young for her."

"Wren's too serious to fuck around with high schoolers."

"She gets it from… fuck if I know. Not me."

"Still itching to get out of Dodge?"

Vee opened a box of painted Santas with a box knife. "Can't blame her for it, you know? I'm glad she wants to do things. Go to college, see the world, all that shit."

"And?"

"And nothing. I'm happy for her."

"Roger that, Vee. Roger that. Swallow that bile."

"I am, thank you."

"You're gonna need to swallow harder," said Paul.

"Don't be gross."

"No, not like that. Have you seen the schedule?"

"No. Do I want to?"

"Probably not, but you're going to see it anyway. Everyone's been cut."

Vee sighed. "Again?"

"Yes, again. I don't make the rules. I guess a Michael's or a Hobby Lobby or something opened. Sales are struggling. We're gonna be lucky if we make it to summer."

"You know, Paul, I think I actually hate it here. You ever hated something before?"

"My ex. But also, yes. I know what you mean. I don't mean it quite as much as you, but I get it."

"You're lucky you married a lawyer."

"Don't I know it."

Faintly, Vee could hear the small crowd outside. Were there more of them now? She watched them with tired eyes and thought about joining them. Whatever was happening there felt infinitely more productive than whatever she was doing at the Mom and Pop Craft Store (soon to be liquidated).

But instead, she shook her head. She drowned it. Another Santa. Another reindeer. Then, eventually, she said, "I'm going to check the schedule."

NINE

Cossel preferred it when he was alone. He did not have to pretend to be okay, nor did he have to pretend he was not okay. He could be himself. His successes were not held against him, nor were his failures. He found, ironically, that they both hurt exactly the same. When he became more stable, more independent—able to walk down the stairs to the fridge—his parents praised him. "He walks! It's a miracle!"

They didn't care that his knee threatened to bend backwards, to slip out of place at every turn. They didn't notice that when he walked, his other leg stepped higher than the other, that he had a limp.

When the doorbell rang, he was able to walk to the door, open it, and welcome Grady inside.

The boy that looked very much like him smiled and feigned sympathy. "Dude, you feeling okay?"

"Yeah, fine," said Cossel. "Little sore. But doing better."

"I heard you couldn't walk."

"You heard wrong, bud."

He looked him up and down, incredulous. "Seriously, you're looking good."

"Thanks, I guess. How are you doing?"

Grady launched into the usual, a run-down of his budding relationship with Erica—a topic that had become the driving narrative of his life so far. Cossel nodded politely through it all, annoyed that the "best thing that ever happened to Grady" coincided with the worst night of his life.

"She's great, dude. So fucking hot."

"Yes," agreed Cossel. "Very pretty."

"She's good for me too. She's been making me a better man." "Yeah?"

"Yeah, dude." Grady turned bright red, despite being clearly eager to share. "She said if I pass my driver's test, I can fuck her in the ass. In the ass, dude! Can you believe that?"

"Just like Romeo and Juliet."

"Right," he said, clearly already stalling out. "She's very sexual. A nympho—she's that kind of chick."

"Great, dude. I'm happy for you."

"Maybe when your leg heals up you can ask Claire or Kayla out or something."

"There's no healing up. The leg is what it is, without surgery."

This was a sticking point with all of his friends and family. They asked if it was better, if he had healed. He was left having to explain that nerve damage doesn't heal. ACLs don't grow back. The leg was fucked. Cossel knew that there was nothing to do, that there was no hope but being cut open.

"Gotcha," said Grady. The information wouldn't stick, it never did. "But you're feeling okay?"

Finally, he'd gotten around it.

"Yes, I'm fine. Doesn't hurt, just hard to walk. I'll be getting more fine as the weeks pass, I think. But not better." Cossel pulled out a rattling prescription bottle. "I'm thinking ten bucks a pill."

"How many are there?"

"Fifteen."

"You want 'em?"

"Well, not me. Erica wants them. But, yeah."

"Cool," said Cossel.

Grady gave him the money in cash and took the pill bottle

as if it were a sort of holy grail. Better than beer, better than weed. The sort of thing that only comes along when the God of Teenage Accidents touches the worthy.

"Thanks," he said. "This is cool. I appreciate it." He looked at the pills and then looked at his friend. "I better be going. Feel better."

"Will do," said Cossel, and soon he was alone again.

There was nothing to do anymore but sleep. He was taking his classes at home now—an indefinitely proposed solution to an indefinitely defined healing period. Part of him wanted to go back, part of him never wanted to see anyone like Grady again.

He pulled out a local automotive classified. On the couch, he looked at cars until he fell asleep. Over the summer, he'd started a lawn mowing business. He'd done what everyone told him he should do. He hustled. For his hustle, he now had $3,000 saved. It was more money than he'd ever had, he was sure that it was more than anyone he knew ever had—except maybe Dom or Kayla.

He dreamed of both of them, in a passing way. They were figures of his subconscious. In his dream, he was back in school. Dom was the teacher now and Kayla and him were both students. Grady was there too, at the back of the class. The class was loud, rowdy. Kayla was the only one paying attention. She sat prim and proper, locking eyes with the newly appointed Mr. Dom. In the dream, Cossel felt unhinged, out of control. He was laughing wildly, throwing wads of paper across the classroom. He kept getting wilder too, wilder and wilder, knowing all well that Dom's eyes were piercing into his back. He could feel his burning stare and in response he allowed himself to become crazier still.

When Cossel woke up, his heart was beating out of his chest. He wished he could pace.

For a moment, he thought he was still dreaming.

The door clicked.

The knob turned.

And he was sure he was going to see Dom. He was sure he was about to be admonished by his enemy. He swallowed to see if he could taste air. He lifted his leg and felt a twinge of pain. *No.*

The door opened.

Cossel got up with a start, then stilled.

His father stood there, a smile on his lips—giddy nervousness dancing in his legs.

"What's up, Dad?" asked Cossel, his words slurred.

"I just got fired," he said.

"What?"

"I'm done. Fired. I need to look for a new job."

Cossel stared at his father, unnerved, waiting for a punchline.

"Why are you smiling?"

"I don't know."

TEN

Wren touched the doorknob and considered turning back from the sliver of a house.

Screaming. There was screaming.

You can leave now, you can disappear. You can jump on a bus and go to fucking New York, Boston. Fuck, Spokane, Boulder. Wherever. You can leave.

She twisted the handle and entered, with the realization that so much of what we do is automation. It happens without thought and when there is thought, it's without resistance. *No choices, forward like a shark*, she thought and opened the door. As she stepped inside, the yelling stopped.

Her father stood on one side of the couch, her mother on the other side, in front of the television. Between them, Cossel was a captive audience.

"Enough. We're not talking about this any longer," said Vee.

"There's nothing to talk about. We'll make it work."

Wren said, "Is there something I should know?"

Her father went to the fridge and for a moment she thought he was going to dodge the question, or worse, let her mother answer it for him. Instead, he cracked open a beer and Mom was silent, as if willing him to talk. "Honey, I lost my job."

"Is that it?"

"That's it."

"That's not it."

"I'll be looking for new opportunities," he said. "In fact, I already found one."

"We need the health insurance, Ed! Don't you understand? Your son is sitting here… he's—"

Ed took a long sip of his beer. "That's going to be taken care of." He sauntered over to his son, nudged him on the shoulder. "We're going to get you your surgery, kid—trust me. We're gonna get you right."

Wren stood like a statue. She felt like she was watching another family's argument. "But?" she asked, extending the syllable.

"But this new opportunity is just a trial thing, it's not forever. But it pays big, we can make a chunk of change and we can use that to invest." His eyes darted to his wife. "If we want."

"What's this big opportunity?"

"I haven't said yet. But it's for all of us," said Ed, calmly. "I was waiting for you to come home."

Wren's mother was crying, but she couldn't tell if she was seriously angry or not. Sometimes she was fake angry, like she just wanted to be heard.

Cossel looked to his sister. "They've been yelling since Mom came home."

"We weren't *yelling*," said Vee.

Wren dropped her bag. "Alright. I'm home now. So what's the big secret?"

Ed settled into the couch. For the first time in a very long time, he had a story. "A coworker told me about this new place," he began. "So, after Kyle unceremoniously dismissed me, I checked it out."

Cormorant/Carmichael was lined with brick, three stories tall. The windows looked like cartoon eyes meant to represent sleepiness. Ed believed that the whole building could fall asleep, given enough time.

It was an office building, but at the front door, all the other names had been scrubbed off. Suites 101 to 315 were occupied by nothing more than residue now. Bits of gunk and plastic. The glass doors that formed its entrance wobbled when pulled. Ed jumped back the first time he pulled on the handle, afraid that he had the wrong place, or worse: that he accidentally broke the door.

On the other side of it was an empty lobby. There was a front desk with no one in it. Behind it, strips of wallpaper hung limp like downed sails. One would expect a building like this, empty and falling apart, to be silent. Ed certainly did. And for his first ten steps into the deserted lobby with no furniture but the front desk, he thought it *was* silent. But his ears adjusted. He listened. Cormorant/Carmichael was anything but silent. It was loud.

A hum, like the sound of industrial machinery reverberated through the walls, punctuated by the sound of steam pistons and metallic clanking. Ed's eyes wandered, drinking in his surroundings. He invested himself in the yellowed walls; the carpeted floor, dotted with oil-black stains. And finally, he saw the hallway of rooms and the door at the end of them. Even from where he was standing, he saw the stairs through the slot of glass embedded at eye level.

He started for them, not entirely sure why. *I could leave at any moment. This place… isn't real.* Ed shook his head. *Why did I think that? What makes a place real? What makes this place unreal?*

Up the stairs—one, two, three flights—no answer. But the hum did vanish. It disappeared into the background. The clanking became no more innocuous than the cars outside. The abandoned vacuum cleaners and sheets of drywall were just scenery. When he reached the top floor, he extended a weak hand toward a swinging door and passed through.

"Good afternoon!"

There was a short wall that took a sharp corner—he peered around it to find a woman smiling behind a desk. Her hair was in a 50s updo. She wore pearl earrings, a blue dress, and had a fake mole drawn on her right cheek. Her smile was straight and perfect.

"Hello," he said.

This lobby was more what he expected. The wallpaper was sickly pink though, which made him nauseous. It smelled generously of perfume—less generously of carrion. The woman who sat behind the desk wore a metal magnetic name tag that read: TRISHA.

Ed realized that she was letting him take it all in, that she was sitting silent while he turned his head. "Sorry," he said.

"Are you here for the job?"

"I don't know," he said. "I guess so. I don't even know what the job is."

She smiled. "We have aptitude tests. Would you like to sit down and take one?"

"Sure," he said. "Do I need to study?"

It was meant as a joke, but Trisha's lips became a straight line. "Please do not study for this test. It's most important that you don't."

"Okay," he said. "That's fine. I won't."

She came around to a door. The desk was really more of a window. "Just come back here, if you please. I'll get you started here. I'm going to show you a video and hand you a piece of paper. You're going to answer the questions and give them to me when you're done. You understand?"

"Understood," said Ed.

He followed her into the backroom, down a narrow corridor lined with Gothic-looking electric lights, each of them a clawed hand holding a fake candle, to a small black room with no windows. In the center of the room was a small, laminated table—the sort in schools and conference rooms the nation over. There was one piece of paper and one pen on top of it. Behind the desk, at the back of the room—that already Ed was beginning to refer to as the "classroom"—there was a projector.

"I haven't seen one of those in years."

Trisha smiled curtly. "Please take your seat."

"Okay," said Ed.

Behind him, the projector whirred to life. He puzzled at the contraption while also not daring to look back, sure that Trisha would come back with a glib rebuke. In front of him, the wall flickered, and just like in the movies, it counted down from ten.

Ed stared straight ahead, unflinching.

"I'll come in when you're done," said Trisha. The lights went out and Ed was all alone in the classroom.

On the screen: a voice, friendly, warm—gravelly. It had the stern, tough, eggs and bacon friendliness of a cowboy. Ed imagined the voice to belong to a man with a mustache. The sort that nodded wisely and laughed at your jokes, that was man enough to handle business, but also accessible enough to share a pitcher of beer with.

"Well, hello there, partner. It seems like you've wandered into the offices of Cormorant/Carmichael. Well, don't worry there, bud. We'll see to it you get what you want, because that's what we're all about here at the old C/C—identifying wants and delivering them to a hungry audience. You're probably wondering now, 'Fella? How can I get my spurs and get in this here business?' And that's a good question, friend. That's a real good question. But first, we need you to answer some questions of our own. Once you do that, we can begin the intake process—if we deem you a quality partner. Sound good, rider? Alright, let's begin."

The voice crooned from behind a black screen, marred with filmic blemishes, the Cormorant/Carmichael logo centered in the middle. Suddenly the screen changed, and the first question appeared.

"What do you want more than anything?" the voice read.

Ed scribbled an answer—a jumble of thoughts. *A house, money, happiness.*

Before he could even finish writing, the next question came up. "Who do you love more than anyone in the world?"

My wife.

Again, the question switched almost as soon as he touched pen to paper.

"Are you religious?"

No.

"Do you have any sexual perversions?"

No.

"When's the last time you've been truly happy?"

Ed's pen hovered above the paper. *I don't know.*

"What's your favorite food?"

Chicken wings.

"What's the worst crime you've ever committed?"

Vandalism.

"Do you have children?"

Yes, two.

"Have you ever had sexual intercourse with either of your children?"

Ed paused. Then, hastily: *NO!!!*

"Where is your dream vacation?"

Private island, a beach.

"If you could kill anyone in the world, who would it be?"

I don't know, no one.

"Where do you see yourself in five years?"

Here.

"Would you say that you are normal?"

Yes.

"You're doing great so far," said the voice. "And we only have one more question. Are you ready?"

Ed found himself mouthing the word 'yes.'

"What would you do if you could do anything?"

Disappear.

The film ran out and the projector continued to whirr. Ed looked at his answers on the sheet and tried to make sense of them. He rubbed his temples. The last ten minutes had been a blur. The door opened and the lights came on.

"How did you do?" she asked.

"Some of the questions there were a little odd."

"Yes, well our research has found them most effective in selecting our candidates. I'm going to take you to another room while Mr. Cormorant studies your results."

She led him back into the hallway where the gothic lightning struck him as strange, but not *as* strange as it once was. Trisha took him into another room. The door had been taken off the hinges. There was a single black leather couch and a potted plant.

"Go ahead," she said. "Take a seat."

Ed sat and waited.

In ten minutes, she returned. "Mr. Cormorant is still analyzing your answers. He requests a little more of your time. This is a thing that he wants."

"Okay," said Ed. "That's fine."

In another fifteen, Trisha came again. She said the same thing and so did Ed.

He couldn't hear the hum in the office anymore. Everything was silent. Peacefully so. The more time he spent in Cormorant/Carmichael, the more he liked it. There was a certain whimsical solitude here. He imagined himself working an office job sometimes and wondered if this was what they were like. He hadn't gone to college and had mostly resigned himself to laboring and working his way up the chain of command, if an organization permitted. In the strange office building, he felt a sense of longing.

When Trisha came back for the third time, she said: "Mr. Cormorant is very impressed with your application. He would like to meet with you."

"I would like to meet with him as well," said Ed.

"Come this way," she said. "He has a proposal."

And Ed followed her down the winding hall, into another office. The whole way he felt as if he were floating.

Ed drank his beer, looked at his family. "It's a one-month gig," he said. "But it involves all of us. Cormorant/Carmichael… the way I understand it… is that they're testing a new product. The product is meant to be a family home—a normal family—and we're that family. I talked with Mr. Cormorant for hours about it. We went over the whole thing. He wants to meet with us. We're going to be a focus group."

Vee wiped her eyes. "A focus group?" It sounded important to her, she liked the idea of it.

"What do we have to do?" asked Vee.

"We have to interact with the product in different ways. I don't know what it means. But he's a nice guy. He said we'll be given instructions."

Cossel nodded. "So, I'm not going to be able to get surgery this month."

"No," said Ed, a defensive edge in his voice. "But it means we'd be able to pay for your surgery. And the ER bill, no problem. He's offering us a lot of money."

"How much?" said Wren. "For all of us? Just you?"

"All of us," said Ed. "This is the best part. They're spending big bucks on this product launch and they want to be sure *everything* works just right. So they're giving us $50,000 each."

Vee, Wren, and Cossel stared at Ed, who for the first time felt the pride of patriarchy. He had hunted, he had gathered. Their jaws fell open. Even the young one seemed to chew on the figure being offered. The numbers flashed in Wren's eyes— it was the sweet sound of escape. For Vee, it was a vacation, a rejuvenating trip.

Ed sat back, smiling ear to ear. "See? One door closes, another one opens. Now, what's for dinner?"

ELEVEN

None of it seemed real until the next day, when each family member woke up, blinked, and tried to remember if they were dreaming or not.

Vee and Ed woke up earliest. They sat at the kitchen table, a yellow legal pad between them. "The ER bill was $500. Surgery is about ten thousand. We could split both of those and still have more than enough to play with," said Vee.

"It won't last forever, but it gives us a year to look for better work."

"I could go to college," said Vee. "I always wanted to."

"Or put down a down payment on a better house."

"That too."

"Vacation."

"Yes. Mexico."

Cossel woke and circled different cars in the magazines. He had been too modest before, he decided. There were better options. He would not be able to afford a nice new car, but there were plenty of nice used ones. He imagined Grady's face when he pulled up to school in a Tesla. Better yet, he imagined Dom's face.

He flipped through the pages and even though he was awake, he was dreaming.

In the shower, Wren let the hot water soak her to the bone. Because she was feeling luxurious, she used every lotion she had.

The water was so hot it was purifying. Like you're removing your outermost layer and the new stuff is pink and bright and stings like Hell, but it's new.

Wren felt new.

But she didn't feel real.

Or rather, *this* didn't feel real.

They were never a rich family, but they had more than when she was a kid. She remembered waking up on Christmas morning, as the first child, and being told that not all families do presents. They had a secondhand plastic tree and cardboard decorations all handmade by her mother. But it was different after Cossel was born. They were only two years apart, but as her memories formed and became clearer, she could remember the stark contrast.

By then, her father had been made assistant manager. Her mother was working full-time at the craft store. They just moved out of a two-bedroom and into the townhouse. It was a paradise for both of them. So grand.

Christmases became grander still. Piles of presents, like there was an element of theater to the entire morning. Whispers of credit card payments after, how one could be skipped and another consolidated. Wren didn't know that her parents weren't well off until she was a teenager and started spending the nights at other kid's houses. Theirs were bigger, of course. They had fewer things, it seemed sometimes. But the things they had were better—more prestigious.

She turned off the water and began drying her hair. She didn't know what any of this meant, but somehow, she knew that it was tinged with sadness.

The heat had fogged up the mirror. The money wouldn't change her parents' life. But maybe, she thought, it could change hers.

"He wants to meet us all," reminded Ed. His family hung on his every word.

"Do we need to dress up?" asked Vee.

"Just look normal. That's all that Mr. Cormorant wants."

Wren's ears perked up. "I've heard that name before. I heard it somewhere."

"Mr. Cormorant?" Vee rubbed her chin. "I saw a man speaking the other day, out in the parking lot. He was surrounded by people. It must have been him."

"I've met him," said Wren, voice iced with smugness. "He was at the diner."

Ed shrugged. "I'm sure Mr. Cormorant has spent a lot of time out in this community." He said it sheepishly, ashamed, as if the wind had just been taken from his sails. "But all the same, he wants to meet with us."

Cossel said, "I think I'm going to ditch the cane today. I don't think I need it." But he was promptly ignored as they talked more about Mr. Cormorant's appearance, his speech, and the strange hold he held over any group.

"My friend, Marta, went to his office. She said he's a magician. Like, an actual magician. An oracle. He lives in like a cave or a coffin or something, she said. She said that he appears to her in her dreams, in her bedroom closet at night, his white face peeking out with a deranged smile. She said that he touched her, like how they do in those weird churches, the megachurches on television—right on the forehead—and suddenly he knew everything about her."

"Is he going to touch us, Ed?"

"I don't know," he said seriously. "He just wants to meet us. That's all I know."

The family tittered about Mr. Cormorant and his minor miracles all the way to the Cormorant/Carmichael office. While at first annoyed, Ed had begun to become very pleased with his wife and daughter's knowledge of Mr. Cormorant.

They made it a lot easier on him. He was afraid that he would have to fight them all the way in. It took no time at all for them to buy into his dream.

Meanwhile, Cossel sat silent in the backseat. Ed stared at him through the mirror and wondered if it was worth a word of reassurance, or if it would only prod the same wound. A simple, "Doing okay back there, bud?" could turn into something much worse these days. So he avoided it. In some ways, he was afraid of his son. Cossel was like him in many ways—painfully average, eager to fit in, vulgar, self-aware—but he possessed something that Ed did not have within him that came to light after his accident—a dash of the erratic. Ed remembered hearing the story of what happened and feeling sick to his stomach, unable to recognize Cossel in the boy that slurred in a drug-induced narrative tucked into a hospital bed. Ed bit his lip, confronting the fact that he and his son were different people.

But Vee and Wren were more like him. Wren had hopes and dreams, so did Vee. They wanted things and were willing to go to conventional lengths to achieve them, and would come up short-handed and wounded if they had to be pushed to unconventional means. He could relate to that all too well.

"Alright, guys. Let's meet the man," he said.

They got out and entered the office. Cossel lingered in the back, slower on his bad leg. Each step he took was so careful it looked as if he was playing a game—avoiding cracks or something like that. Meanwhile, the other three forged ahead—Ed once again reclaiming leadership of the group with the running tally of his experience.

"It's up on the top floor," he said. "I had to really search for it this time."

"Oh, I wonder if they're remodeling," mused Vee.

"I bet they're turning it into one of those, like, tech company offices. Open floor plans, windows, pool table."

"Could be," said Ed.

No one saw Cossel's eyes water when he looked up. "No one told me there'd be stairs," he mumbled.

The rest of his family traversed them with audible wonder, leaving Cossel bracing with each step, holding onto the bannister with a death grip. He flexed his leg muscles, tight and hard, with each step to protect his knee. Once, somewhere on the second flight, his rhythm was disturbed by his father's words. "Everyone: listen. Can you hear that hum?"

Cossel tried to hear the hum while relearning to walk with a floppy foot and a floating knee, and his leg bent backward at the joint and he found himself falling forward and lifting to correct it. He gasped suddenly. The stops had been pulled out of his leg, it threatened to bend *all the way back*. He cringed at the thought.

Statue still, he stood in his corrected position and took inventory of his body. Nothing had happened. He was safe.

He took a breath and continued.

His family had been replaced by the hum. He could not see them, and he could not hear them.

"Hey guys, wait up," he said. "Wait up, I almost tripped."

Silence.

He took each step as if it were Everest itself, and when he finally reached the top stair, his family was already standing in the lobby.

"I'm here," he said.

Ed turned to his son and gave him a curt nod. "It's just gonna be a second. They're alerting Mr. Cormorant to our arrival."

"Got it," said Cossel.

Wren took a step back. She put an arm around her little brother and squeezed him. Cossel leaned into it.

"So bro, what are you going to do with your money?"

Cossel was in a void, a thousand miles away. Cold loneliness crept into him. He might as well have been at the bottom of the ocean. The woman in the lobby appeared in front of him, and she might as well have been speaking from a different galaxy, her words traveling across icy space on the wings of light and sound. "Come this way," she said. "The Psychographist will see you now."

TWELVE

The office was an exploration of maximalism. The walls were covered in photos, dozens of them framed in different sizes—black and white and color alike—from floor to ceiling. The furniture was mismatched. Ed sat in a plush, red Victorian chair with a high back and ornately carved armrests. Vee sat in a plastic chair with four metal legs. Wren sat in a minimalist silver half-orb. Cossel sat unsteadily on a wooden bar stool. Across from them, there was a large oak desk. This desk was even *more* intricately carved. And not just the sides, but the top too. It was a tableau of roaring lions, knights, dragons, caskets, saints, and virgins. Medieval, perhaps—or at least an impression of medieval woodcuts. It was so carved up though, that it ceased to function reasonably as a desk. Cossel imagined trying to sign a simple paper on it and having the pen stab through into the carved grooves behind it.

Interestingly too, despite the ready assortment of chairs, the man across from them did not sit in a chair. The desk was raised on stacks of old books and the man behind it stood. It came up to the top of his stomach and he looked rather like a judge with the desk so high. As if he were looking at the Hoyers and about to make a pronouncement.

The family sat still, waiting for the man to speak. They studied his pallor, his black suit, his healthy roundness, his lipstick-red lips, his dagger of a widow's peak, and the shark-like black of his small, round eyes.

Finally, he said, "You are the Hoyers. My name is Cormorant. I am what they call a psychographist. It is a pleasure to meet you."

"Nice to see you again, Mr. Cormorant. May I introduce you to my family?"

"No, no. Please, don't," said the Psychographist. "Allow me." He came around the table and revealed that he was also wearing shiny black shoes.

"Ed, we have already met. A good man, a normal man. One who wants to do best by his clan. You are a hungry dog chewing through the walls of what has been given to you. Yes, I see it all too well, beyond and through." He walked along toward Vee, two steps that were taken in the space of eons. He squinted slightly, turning his shark eyes into tiny black hyphens. "And here is Vee. Wife of Ed. Darling, I've heard so much about you. Sad, fraught—in this life you have been caught. A rabbit snared, yipping helplessly while the hangman stares. There is no escape, only a long slow circle around the drain."

Two more steps. "Wren, lovely to meet you. The daughter of two would-be escapees. It only makes sense that you too would flee. It will be my pleasure to fund that endeavor."

Two more steps and he was in front of Cossel.

"Dear Cossel," he said. "I've heard so much about you. I'm sorry to hear about your accident. It's not good for a boy to be so injured, and even I am not inured to your pain. But also, I am glad you are here with us today. If there's anything I can do to help you, please let it be known." He cocked his head at him. "A boy like you… oh what does a boy like you want? Ah, of course. A car. Yes, a car. A reasonably priced, yet extravagantly nice car."

When his introductions were finished, he glided back around to his desk. "I trust Ed has filled you in on the details."

"Only partially. I think it'd be best if we heard it from you."

"And we want a contract," said Vee.

Mr. Cormorant nodded. "Yes, of course. Well, allow me to make the offer officially. Cormorant/Carmichael wants to use you as the subjects of an extended focus group. You will be testing a new, yet-to-be-named product. For the purposes of this conversation, we will simply call it the Product. You will live in your home for one month, without leaving—although you can have visitors. You will use the product as we tell you to, performing tests and providing reactions and commentary as deemed necessary. Each week, I will visit and interview you as a group. This will last for four weeks. When our research period ends, we will remove the product from your home and you will each receive $50,000, a total of $200,000, in one payment by check or direct deposit—your choosing. Are there any questions?"

Wren asked, "What sort of product is the Product?"

"Part of the agreement is not knowing, I'm afraid. We want blind reactions," said Mr. Cormorant.

"What about food? What about bills?" asked Vee. "We can't leave the house for a month?"

"Our organization will pay your bills and provide you food for the month you stay with the Product."

"What about school?" asked Cossel.

"I'm afraid you will have to miss it. Or do your schoolwork from home. Given your situation though, I don't think that will be a problem, will it?"

"I got an email the other day asking me when I'd be back," lied Cossel.

The Psychographist grinned. "Is that so?"

"Yes."

"In that case, perhaps you can hold them off a little longer. One month isn't so long. You can say you tripped climbing these stairs, perhaps?"

Cossel felt as if he'd been punched in the stomach.

"Are there any other questions?"

Ed said, "What is a psychographist?"

Mr. Cormorant nodded, smirking, as if he was in on a history of secrets no one knew but him. "Are you aware of the field of psychographics?"

"No."

"Psychographics is the study and implementation of psychology and marketing. Consumer personas, you might say. It's a key part of any strategy to understand one's customer. If you go to a Wal-Mart, do you have an image of the type of person who shops there? What about a Target? You might have two different people in mind—even if some people shop at both. This is a consumer persona. The type of person who buys your product. I am a practitioner of this, a skilled one you might say. More skilled than the rest. In fact, I'm the only person I know who has turned this key part of product launch and strategy into a profession all its own. As far as I know, there are no other Psychographists but myself."

"So why are you running this?" asked Cossel, perhaps too hastily.

"Excuse me?"

"You're the guy who says this product is for these people or that product is for those people. You already know who the product's for. Why are you testing it on us?"

"Good business is done with good testing, my boy," he said. "Even I have been mistaken. But also, what's the point in making a guess if you never find out if you're right?"

This all made sense to the family. The Hoyer's didn't question the strange pale man that stood in front of them, behind the innately carved desk.

"I'm going to need you to sign these contracts, of course," said Mr. Cormorant, his ruby red lips pursed as if poised to kiss. "Please feel free to read them over, sign them, and return them to me, now."

He handed out four clipboards. Not one of them read the piece of paper in front of them. They didn't have to. There was only one line highlighted on each page and it was a big one. *$50,000.*

Each of them signed and returned the page.

Ed sighed, as if refreshed from a brisk dunk in icy water.

"Alright, then," he said. "So when do we start?"

Mr. Cormorant examined each signature, tracing the lines with his long fingers as if he were memorizing their loops and curves. He looked up at them and blinked his shark eyes. "Tomorrow," he said. "Tomorrow."

THIRTEEN

It was like Christmas morning, not the kind Wren remembered—the sparse ones tinged with social sorrow and jealousy. But the ones Cossel remembered. Presents, colors, anticipation, running down the narrow townhouse stairs when he was still small enough to think of it as big. He didn't know anything about fake trees or real trees back then. They were all green and perfect.

He awoke early and went downstairs, now aware of his own excitement and working to curb it as much as possible. He remembered his age, his appearance, his leg, and suddenly excitement was something to be tamped down and diminished. Therefore, by the time he reached the bottom step, he wore a face of boredom marked with considerable angst. It was something he had practiced.

His mother, father, and sister were already up. And to his surprise, Mr. Cormorant was standing in the center of his living room. To even more surprise, Dom stood beside him.

Cossel went rigid on the bottom step, and then gracefully recovered, his face a mask. He worked hard to care as little as he could about the dark, curly-haired boy with the broad shoulders in his living room.

Out of the corners of his eyes, Dom seemed to be of the same mind. He was holding onto the top of a heavy blue dolly, where he had apparently just deposited a large heavy cardboard box. He seemed smaller now, in his living room, less lively, less quick with a jab.

Cossel joined his family on the couch silently, his eyes shifting between Dom and Mr. Cormorant.

"Ah good, you're awake," said the Psychographist. "We're happy to have you here. I believe you've met my assistant, young Dominic."

Both Cossel and Dom nodded toward each other.

"Very good, very good. So here we have the Product. It's what we've all been waiting for. This is the prototype. Dom, please, go ahead and cut open the box."

Dom retrieved a box knife from his pocket and joylessly went about cutting open the box. With some effort, he rocked a large black object out of its cardboard confinement and placed it on the floor. With a final effort, he pulled the bubble wrap sleeve off the top of it and took a step back.

Cossel looked on, puzzled.

The device had nothing in common with anything he'd ever seen. It was about four and a half feet tall, black, and long and thin, almost needle-like at the point, with a flared base. Cossel thought, for a moment, that it was a tiny skyscraper model, reduced to the size of a small youth. Only, it wasn't really that. It cinched in various portions like links of sausages, but sharp and angular. It wasn't symmetrical either, with some sharp outcroppings occurring at various parts of its length. In the middle, or near the middle at least, there was a long line of LEDs that emanated clean, emerald light.

"This here," said Mr. Cormorant, "is our Product. What do you think?"

"It's beautiful," said Vee.

"Very interesting," said Ed.

It was Wren who asked what Cossel was already thinking. "What does it do?"

"That is for you to find out, and for us to observe."

Cossel chimed in. "Okay, then. But then what *do we do*?"

"Go about your lives as normal," said Mr. Cormorant. "Eat, talk, be merry. Whatever that means to you. Play games. Read. Dance. Learn an instrument. Fuck. Whatever it means to you."

Cossel sat uncomfortably. He and all the rest of his family's eyes were glued to the Product. He noticed though, in an attempt to look away from its glow, that Dom was looking at his shoelaces.

"I must bid you farewell, fair Hoyers," said Mr. Cormorant. "I will be checking in on you periodically. Please be well!"

And just like that, the Psychographist left, as had Dom.

Cossel sat in front of the Product and wondered what it meant, what it could do. But mostly, he thought about his fifty-thousand dollars, and what he could do with that.

FOURTEEN

The first day with the product was like any other day. Or rather, it was like any other day that the Hoyers spent alone together. They fought and argued like a normal family. They also simmered and made jokes like a normal family. They watched television, made dinner, talked about their days, and glanced at the Product as a group. It was there and they could not help but look at it.

But they did this all as they always would.

That first night, however, there was one bit of strangeness.

They did not know it, but they all dreamed the same dream.

All four of them woke at the same time, starting up in bed and stifling a scream. Only Vee and Ed had any inkling that the dream was a shared experience, because they woke and looked at each other with a slow dawning realization. Although, neither of them made this realization explicit. It was dark, there was no moon.

Ed simply said, "Sorry, I had a bad dream."

"Yes, me too."

And then they settled back into bed.

Of course, they couldn't fall asleep.

So, then, Vee's hand crept onto Ed's leg and then slowly reached up to his cock. Ed's hand reached over to her thighs, then her breasts, and soon they were both moaning. As Ed got on top of her, he realized they hadn't made love in weeks, if not longer. But Ed was an animal and this thought didn't persist. In some men, it might open a wound, a sad acknowledgment of the state of his marriage, but Ed did not think like that. He lived in the present and was happy to be loved in the present, if not in the past.

He pumped into her enthusiastically. Vee moaned in celebration. She had not been fucked in a long time and was glad that it was happening now. There would be no way to go back to sleep after what they saw in their dream either. When she came, she did not think about being swallowed by a giant maw of sharpened white teeth. She thought of Ed, who was barreling toward his orgasm, and soon would be dripping out of her.

When they finished, they held each other, closed their eyes, and pretended to believe that what had happened in their heads was gone now. That it didn't bother them anymore. But it did, of course.

Below them, their children masturbated sleepily to the rhythms of their lovemaking.

Wren in one room, Cossel in another. Neither of them *knew* that that was what they were doing, but it was what was done all the same.

Wren thrashed in her blankets, assuring herself that there was nothing wrong with self-pleasure. That she was not masturbating *to* her parents, but it was just a coincidence that they were orgasming at the same time. She assured herself that she was mature enough to shrug off this strange behavior.

And Cossel did much the same. *Teenagers jack off all the time*, he told himself. He was not thinking about his mother's moans when he released into his sheets. He was not thinking about how his father was pinning his mother to the bed and searching desperately for his own orgasm. This was unfortunate timing, but really, there was nothing else to do.

After the entire family had cum, they all settled into their own nest of musk and ejaculate. They hugged themselves, in the absence of another. But most of all, they were sure that the dream was nothing of importance.

FIFTEEN

When Cossel peeled the blanket off of himself and saw the remnants of his ejaculate, now dried like snakeskin, gluing his dick to his sheets, he felt a wave of shame. Some teenagers feel intense shame from masturbation, despite talking about it endlessly. Cossel was one of them. He aspired to a sort of stoicism about sexuality that came from a fear of being wrong. Even alone, covered in his own semen, he had the distinct feeling that there was no one else who did the things he did to himself. That for everyone else, self-pleasure was a sort of comical hypothetical, and that they only joked about it the way people joked about car wrecks or zombie apocalypses.

Cossel couldn't shake this truth, so he hid his pleasure from himself. He stripped nude and threw the lock to his door. Hurriedly, he changed his clothes. There was no sense in dismaying too outwardly, as that was also something he feared mockery for. The only thing a man should do is face problems with the plain bored face of an efficient automaton.

New clothes fitted onto his body and the problems of the night disappeared. He resolved silently to not be taken by his own pleasure so much, lest it be in the warm embrace of a wanting woman.

He stayed in his room for a little longer still, booting up his computer to play an online game. He took the reins of a mean-faced space marine and blasted apart aliens, reducing them to screaming masses of jellied blood. To go down too soon would be to run from himself, he was sure.

Grady's name popped up at the bottom of his screen.

Do you have any more pills?

Cossel sighed. He clicked on the message, typed.

Dude. Don't say that kinda shit on here.

Sorry. Sorry. Just wanted to know if you had any more lol.

Nope. Fresh out. That was my last refill.

Awwwwww

Yep.

Okay but we were rolling last night. Can I video call you?

Cossel acquiesced to his friend. He opened the video chat and quickly ran a finger through his hair. Grady's face popped up and Cossel was sure more than ever that they were the same boy.

"Okay, dude. I need more," he said. "That shit is so good."

"Well, yeah. It's not made in a bathtub."

"You think you can get some more?"

"Probably not," said Cossel. "I'm not even walking with a cane anymore. So everyone thinks I'm better."

Grady gave a thumbs up and Cossel immediately regretted sharing this with him. "Dude, does that mean you're gonna go for soccer next year?"

"I can't," he said. "Not without surgery."

"When are you getting surgery?"

"Soon, maybe. I don't know. It's expensive…"The urge to impress a peer reached its breaking point and Cossel cursed his break from Stoicism. "We might be coming into some money now."

"Fuck, yeah?"

"Fuck yeah."

"What does that mean?"

Cossel told Grady the story in as few words as possible. "It's a focus group thing, but it's like this huge company… or it must be at least. It's a huge thing."

"God, are they hiring?"

"They hired Dom," said Cossel.

"Dom? Ha, that's wild. You heard he and Kayla broke up?"

"I didn't know they were together."

"They certainly knew each other *very* well."

"Why'd they break up?"

"No idea. You interested to swoop in there and get some of that pu-*ssay*?"

"No," said Cossel. "Just curious. Dom was at my house yesterday, with Mr. Cormorant."

Grady's eyes lit up. "Ohhh, that guy."

"You know him?"

"Of him. Everyone knows about that guy. Or at least a little bit. I've seen him out there, like, preaching. He was talking in rhymes. What the fuck is up with that? Does he do that all the time?"

"No, not all the time. But yeah, sometimes. It's fucking weird," he admitted.

"My parents talk about him all the time. Dom does too."

"You hang out with Dom?"

"Yeah," said Grady. "But we're not really friends. He's kind of a dick. Really competitive. Erica and Kayla were friends and that's why we hung out, but now he's not around and I don't have any reason to see him—so that's kind of a plus, right?"

"Yeah, I guess. He looked bummed as all hell when I saw him. Torn up." Cossel relished having something to add to the story.

Grady laughed. "I don't know what happened but I heard it was a fucking blowout. Screaming, shouting—*I'll never speak to you again* shit."

"Where did it happen?"

"In *school*."

"Oh shit. So everyone saw it. That's gnarly," he said. Cossel liked this, he felt at ease again, like this was normal. Also though, he was sorry that he was so out of the loop. "I've been a bit of a hermit, I guess. I'm missing out."

"When are you coming back? We miss you. We can sign your cast or some shit."

"I don't have a cast. You know that. You saw me the other day."

"I know, I know."

"I'll be back next month. In one month, I guess. They keep letting me work at home, it's nice though."

"Lucky. You get to just jack off every day, huh?"

Cossel laughed uncomfortably. "No, afraid not." He deflected. "My parents and sister are here too. It's not quite that free of an environment. But I should be able to get a car soon." This was the turn of the tide, where Cossel went on the attack. "You going to get your license anytime soon?"

"Yeah, yeah," said Grady, his eyes darting to another screen. "Soon."

From there, the conversation petered out. All conversations, and especially this one, were a transaction, an exchange. One offered something and the other one countered. They both left with a precious commodity. Here, the goal was that what the other left with would be a devaluing element. If either had done their job, the other would walk away with a wound. The wound would fester, grow worse throughout the day. In the middle of the night, it would speak to them. It would whisper: *you are not good enough* and it would do so ad infinitum, pushing them to a painful new reality where those words become true.

As each had their own private wounds, as each would not be able to acknowledge, they ended the call with friendly goodbyes. The jockeying was done. It was time to go to the trough.

Downstairs, his parents were on the couch, watching television. They laid in each other's arms in a way he had not seen them do, ever. The Product sat in the corner, its LED strip glowing.

"Has it done anything yet?" asked Cossel.

"Nope," said Vee. "Nothing except change color. I think we're being pranked."

"Easiest money we've ever made," said Ed, a smile on his lips. He rubbed at his goatee, adjusted his glasses. "I think we just got ourselves a stay-cation. What have you been doing this morning, Cos?"

"Played video games, talked with Grady."

"Anything going on with him?"

"Not really. Same," he said. "Where's Wren?"

"Upstairs," said Vee. "Probably talking to a friend or something." She closed her eyes slowly, savoring it. "I'm pretty sure it can't get much better than this."

"What's for dinner?" asked Cossel.

"Hold your horses, kid," said Vee. "We're having lunch first. Croque Monsieur's. You know what that is? That's a French grilled cheese sandwich. They're fancy. Mr. Cormorant sent us groceries."

"We never have lunch."

"We have the time now," said Ed. "Get used to it. This is luxury, my man."

Cossel nodded. "I guess so. I think I'll go see what's Wren doing. Or maybe play a video game."

"Sounds good, dude," said Ed.

Cossel twisted too soon though and he felt his knee slip. He cursed himself, his haste, and went upstairs. Stairs had slowly become a silent, taunting enemy. He resolved to ask his mother if she could bring his meals up to his room lest he tempt fate.

He knocked on Wren's door. "Are you decent?" he asked.

"Yeah, come in."

He pushed the door open. Wren was on her bed, laying back, her legs crossed in black sweats covered in splotches of rust-colored bleach stains. "What's up?" she asked.

"Nothing, bored," he said.

"Yeah? You can do anything you want. Do it."

"I can't do anything I want. I can do anything I want inside this house. Meanwhile, there's that dumb block of black plastic down there. What is this bullshit?"

"My ticket to an out-of-state school," said Wren. She dropped her phone to her side. "How's the leg, bro?"

"Shit sucks, like usual." Cossel felt a closeness with his sister he didn't feel with anyone else in his family, he felt relief at being able to express negative emotion to her.

"Sorry, Cos," she said. "It's not hurting though, right?"

"No. I'm just tired of Mom and Dad pussy-footing around surgery."

"Oh God, if you leave it up to them, they'll make excuses forever. Do you know how long it took me to get their financial information for college? I had to fight them day after day for it. Eventually, I just looked up their tax forms on Dad's computer. He doesn't even keep the thing locked."

"That would fucking suck," said Cossel.

"It would. But that's par for the course. This place sucks. But, with this money..." Cossel spotted a vicious glint in Wren's eye. "They might just make you pay for it yourself."

"They wouldn't do that."

"They *would*."

Cossel shook his head. "We don't even have insurance now. Wouldn't that be like *really* expensive."

"Probably. But Dad's lost so much money on crypto, they don't have shit for savings. Mom is dying looking at all her friends going to the Bahamas every Christmas. I wouldn't be surprised if they blow it all in a couple months."

Her words felt like daggers. "If that happens, I'm gonna blow my brains out."

"No, you won't," she said. "There's no point. You only got two more years. As soon as you turn eighteen, run the fuck away."

"I will," he said, not sure if he meant it. "But where do I go?"

"College."

"But what if I don't want to go to college? I'm average as fuck."

"Of course you are. Most people are. I am too. That doesn't mean shit. Lots of idiots get degrees."

"Ha, thanks."

"No, really. Or go into a trade school. There's nothing keeping you from it. Or hell, just move away. Get out of Springfield."

"All my friends are here." Even as he said it though, he had to laugh.

"You really planning on seeing Grady for the rest of your life? You gonna be old men together?"

"No," he admitted. "I'm not even sure if I really like him these days."

Wren smiled. "Yeah, bro. Went through the same thing. Remember Lara?"

"No."

"Well, I do. She was a cunt. We smoked together, a lot. Like all the time. Black light posters, beads hanging from the doorways. All that shit. Then, she started becoming one of those 'weed is medicine' people. She kept saying dumb shit, getting mad at people who called it a drug, or who pointed out that she literally did nothing else but smoke weed and talk about weed and go on weed forums to make weed friends. I'm not saying it's bad, it's not. It's fucking fun. Of course it is, but it's one of those things that gives you an immediate feel-good, and sometimes we don't need an immediate feel-good. Everything around us is trying to become that, an instant way for dopamine to be released or whatever. Weed is an easy, safe way to get that hit."

"So she got annoying and you bounced?"

"Well, the medicinal weed shit got out of control. Of course, weed is medicine for some people. But I'm not talking about glaucoma. I'm talking weed for the common cold, cancer, et cetera. If Lara had seen your injury she would've smoked you out and told you that's all you need. But of course she would. She was an idiot."

Cossel nodded, not sure what he was supposed to take from this. "Do you ever see her now?"

"Nope, couldn't if I wanted to. She swallowed two bottles of aspirin and died in a bathtub a year ago."

"Is this some sort of big sister anti-drug talk?"

"No. Well, kind of. Maybe. I don't know. I don't think it was the weed that killed her or made her kill herself. That's a dumb thing to think and I don't subscribe to that Protestant anti-drug shit. But I think she was the type of person who needed to feel good. And you can only outrun that for so long."

"I wanna feel good," said Cossel. "What's wrong with that?"

"Who doesn't? But you gotta take the good with the bad. You ever think about how shit was two thousand years ago? No phones, no constant information. Entertainment was crude and meant to be savored. Isn't that insane? Advertisements existed, but they did not demand your attention. Your attention right now is commodified. Think about that."

"I don't know what you're saying."

"What are we being paid to do right now?"

"Stand around the Product."

"Right. We're giving our attention to this thing for money. Why? Who the fuck cares. Also, imagine a life where that's *never* a thing. Can you even picture it? There are no ads on mobile games, no product placement in movies, no one tracking your every move, no archetypes to aspire to. You think I want to go to college, or do you think I want to be the type of person who went to college? Take a guess, kiddo. Everything that we are is the product of Products."

Cossel took a step back from his sister. She was different. Her voice cracked when she spoke. "I don't know what you're trying to tell me, Wren. Are you okay?"

Wren shook her head. "Sorry, I'm feeling odd. Maybe I'm getting into my late capitalist feminist shrew phase. I'm just tired, that's all. Hey, can I ask you a question?"

Cossel shrugged. "Sure," he said. "What's up?"

"I don't know, nothing. I don't think so at least. But I was wondering…" She took a deep breath. "Did you hear anything last night?"

A huge cosmic mouth might as well have opened in the room and sucked the air into its galactic lungs. Cossel froze.

"I don't know," he said. "I don't think so."

Wren smiled at him, a wan confusing smile that made him feel weak. "That's good," she said. "That's probably for the best."

SIXTEEN

Vee spent the afternoon cooking, which she found herself enjoying. She kept saying the word housewife, as if she was afraid no one else would say it. "Aren't I just a cute little housewife?" she'd say. Or, "Ed, how do you like having a housewife?"

Other times, she'd allude to it without making it explicit. "Do you think I should get one of those cute 50s dresses? Maybe put my hair up?"

Every time, Ed found a new delight in this. He'd smile and put his hands on her hips and pull her toward him until their waists touched and then kissed her on the mouth.

Vee also liked this touch and if she were to think about it, she wouldn't have remembered when they were last like this. Secretly, she thought it was the Product. That it was dispensing some sort of friendly pheromone. Whatever it was, she approved.

After lunch, she washed the dishes and suddenly Ed was behind her, whispering into her ear. "Do you wanna go upstairs for a little?" he asked, his erection fighting through the fabric of his sweats.

Her breath hitched and an aching heat overcame her. "Again?"

"Again," he said.

"What about the kids?"

"They don't need us. They're fine."

"What if they hear?"

"They won't," he said.

She smiled and they crept up the stairs like a pair of naughty kids. When they reached the bedroom and closed the door behind them, Ed's hands were all over her. He stripped her down and kissed her hard on the lips. She kissed him back. She stroked his cock. He rubbed her clitoris. In bed, they fucked in the missionary position and they both orgasmed, just as they were told they should.

After, they laid in bed, staring up at the ceiling.

Ed said, "Do you hear that?"

"What?" asked Vee.

"A hum. I didn't notice it till now."

Vee listened. She *did* hear it. Ever so slightly. A ringing tuning fork stuck deep within the walls. "Yeah," she said. "Just barely."

"Do you think it's that thing down there? The Product?"

"It must be," she said. "I can't think of what else it'd be. I didn't hear it make a hum yesterday."

"It sounds like the office building. They must have made it there," he said. Ed thought about this for a moment. Then said, "I suppose we'll get used to it."

"Yes. We will. It's a small price to pay," she said. She rolled over. "Do you have any more cigarettes?"

"Cigarettes?"

"I could smell them on you the other day. Don't hold out on me. I'm not mad," she said.

Ed stretched and got out of bed. "Only if you're not mad."

"I haven't smoked for years. Since high school. I miss it, you know. I've always wanted to have one after sex, like in the movies."

He reached into the closet. "Almost a full pack," he said. "Should I open a window?"

Vee rolled over onto her stomach. Her skin was smooth. Ed thought, right then, that she was beautiful. More so than when he first met her. "No," she said. "I don't think so. It's cold, isn't it? I don't want to be cold when I smoke. I want to be warm."

He pulled out a smoke for himself and put one between her lips. He lit them both with a gas station lighter. They both inhaled deeply. "This is great," he said. "This is wonderful."

The nicotine entered his veins and a pleasure center went off. It electrified his brain and he almost gasped. It was a whisper of an orgasm. His toes curled, slightly. He swallowed. "Jesus, that's a good cigarette."

"It is," purred Vee. "I never knew a smoke could be so fucking good. Where did you get these?"

"The gas station by my work. They're just normal cigarettes. Cheap, even."

"Huh," she said. "They taste great."

"Everything tastes great when you don't have to work," he said.

Vee took another long drag of her smoke, and Ed did too. "It's sad, almost, that we only have another month of this. It's going to fly by so fast."

"But the money."

"Yes," he said. "The money."

In his room, Cossel listened to music. He stayed hidden. He burned through food that he was surprised to have seen his mother made. She did not typically make great food. But that didn't mean she was a bad cook. Usually, she was tired. Or stressed. Cossel managed to forget about his leg in his room. Music thumped in his ears and he could not hear his parents have sex, nor could he remember the conversation his sister had with him earlier.

All was good for the Hoyers. They were beginning to loosen up.

SEVENTEEN

Mr. Cormorant came after one week, on the dot. He was alone this time, a fact that Cossel found pleasing. He did not want to see Dom, but if he did, he thought he might call him out on his bullshit. His tough guy bullshit. His alpha male macho bullshit. Cossel smiled at that idea. He often imagined ripping Dom's teeth out one by one. Slitting his throat. Removing his organs.

Cossel was feeling free. He did not run down the stairs, but he walked quickly down them. It was closer to a run than he had attempted in a while. It was close enough to call it a win.

Wren gave him a hug, kissed him on the cheek when he came down. "Nice moves, bro," she said.

"Thank you, thank you," he said. "I used to be a track star, you know?"

They laughed at that.

In the living room, none of them wore anything but sweats and T-shirts. Wren and Vee had taken to going braless.

Mr. Cormorant said, "How are the Hoyers today? A week has passed and now we must talk. What can you tell me about your week?"

Vee shrugged. "Nothing, really. We've just been chilling, I guess. It's been nice being a family again."

Mr. Cormorant nodded, smiling. "Very good. How has the Product been?"

"It hums," said Ed. "But that's it."

"Have you noticed anything about it?"

Cossel and Wren shook their heads.

Ed and Vee giggled.

"Parents? Is there something you want to share with the class?" asked Mr. Cormorant with a smile.

"It's just—" Ed shook his head. "No really, we shouldn't."

"We've been more intimate lately," said Vee. "That's all. As a married couple."

Cossel laughed. "So, that's what you kids are doing up there all the time."

"Guilty," said Ed.

"At least they're spending time together," said Wren. "If I was alone with my husband all the time, I'd wanna fuck too."

The conversation came easily. Cossel felt warm in the home, free to be himself. He stretched and yawned and laughed with his family. "I'm just glad someone's getting laid," he said.

They all joined in on this laughter. It was really very good.

"Besides the increase in fuckery, have you noticed anything else?" asked Mr. Cormorant.

"I don't think so," said Ed. "It hums though. That's about it. But I can't hear it anymore."

"Ah yes, it does produce a low frequency hum. But as you said, it disappears in no time. There is no reason or rhyme to it. It is but a product of the machine, of how whatever inside of it has been captured and caught. So, do not fret. There is nothing to worry about. For the next week, now that we have a baseline, we will be making some changes to this whole affair." The Psychographist pulled a remote from his long wool overcoat and pressed a button. The Product's LED changed from green to orange.

Cossel blinked. He liked it. It looked pleasing. He said as much. The family all agreed.

"This week, I have three challenges for you. These are tasks for you to complete. First, I would like you all to play a game together. All of you. It doesn't matter what game, only that you play it together in the house."

"Board game? Video game?" asked Ed.

"It doesn't matter," said Mr. Cormorant. "Second, I'd like you to have a conversation with someone from outside the home. Via telephone or another long-distance method. I don't want you to leave the house or invite anyone over, yet. This is to remain your domain. Third, I'd like you to try something you've never done before."

Cossel nodded, trying to search his brain for something he hadn't done, but wanted to do. But the softness of his mind assured him nearly immediately, that it needn't be something he *wanted* to do.

Mr. Cormorant clasped his hands. "One last thing," he said. "You might hear the Product speak to you this week. It might ask you to do additional tasks. Please carry them out without fuss."

The door opened and Cossel couldn't tell if Mr. Cormorant even reached out a hand to touch it. It just seemed to fly open and the man in the black passed through the entryway, and just like that it closed behind him again. *Huh*, he thought. *Curious.* But the idea was easy to let go. It appeared and vanished like so many of his other thoughts, as did the Psychographist.

EIGHTEEN

At the start of the second week, an uneasy despair set in.

"It already feels like it's gonna be over," said Vee. "So soon."

"I don't even care about the money," said Ed. "I just want to stay home and fuck."

They looked to Wren and Cossel, who were both on their phones. Each scrolled through images, videos, text, allowing each one to poke and prod and satiate their brains. They couldn't hear their parents, but even if they could, they would not care. It had become a curious development in the household, this new openness. The Hoyers were never prudes, but like most Americans, they did not parade their sexuality. When Wren and her friends talked about sex, they often discussed it without ever saying the word. With Cossel, the conversation used to be especially painful. His whole body would cringe when his parents came into his room to discuss his body and its changes. Even with Grady, they would talk privately of "hooking up," but not fucking.

Sex was a private matter that should stay private, but now, they had loosened up on that. They made no euphemisms of what pleasure they sought. The day before, Cossel announced that he was going to go up to his room.

His mother asked, "What are you gonna do?"

And without a thought, he said, "Probably jack off for a little bit."

They all laughed at this, especially Cossel—who even apologized. But Vee, tears in her eyes, explained it wasn't necessary. When Cossel came back downstairs they asked him how it was. He told them it was excellent. Wren then went upstairs, saying, "Guess it's time for me to clock in," with a wink.

Sex and pleasure were no longer conversations to be avoided.

"This is what they call utopian," said Wren at one point.

Her father snorted. "What's that?"

"Like a perfect world or something. It's the type of world we all build toward. Something idealistic."

He mulled that over for a moment. "I guess it is that, isn't it? God, what I wouldn't do for some ass. Vee?"

"Are you speaking literally or figuratively? You can fuck my pussy if you want, but I don't do anal. Not my thing."

"Have you ever tried it?"

"Yeah, with Craig."

Wren laughed. "Oooh, who's Craig?"

"My high school boyfriend before your father. It fucking hurt."

Ed's face went dour. "I didn't know you did anal with him."

She shrugged. "I didn't think it was a big deal. I didn't like it."

Ed, for a moment, seemed to stare off into space.

Wren's smile twisted outward. "Oh shit, Dad, are you jealous of Craig?"

Vee doubled over on the couch as Ed's lips became tighter. Cossel howled with laughter.

"Oh honey, don't be like that. It was nothing. It was nothing at all."

"Grady's girlfriend is gonna let him fuck her in the ass, she said," offered Cossel. "Maybe one day her husband will be butthurt over it too!"

That too made them cry out in laughter.

"I don't think it's funny," said Ed.

"You can fuck my pussy, if you want," said Vee. "You can go upstairs and fuck it right now. Will that make you feel better?"

"I'm not in the mood anymore. It's fine. Let's not talk about it anymore."

They did fuck though, because Cossel could hear them. They fucked savagely, so unhinged was their fucking that they didn't even bother to close the door to their bedroom. Cossel heard them that night and masturbated again, this time unashamed of where or why he was masturbating. He matched his rhythm to the clanking of the bed frame.

Downstairs, the Product continued to glow.

As his cum came out in staccato spurts, he was thankful that his father and mother were fucking. *We're a real happy family*, he thought. *This is how happy families should behave. We want things and we take them.*

And that thought would last for a moment or two. Maybe even a day.

But they hadn't yet had to play a game.

Wren was the first to bring it up. "So, I know everybody is busy eating and cumming, but we have shit to do this week."

Ed nodded. "That's right. We need to play a game, right?"

"That's right," said Vee.

They all were in the living room, all were staring at the Product and its orange glow. The lights were off, and its small light bathed them, highlighting their creases and turning their eyes into black sockets.

"We surely have a board game. We could play Life. Or Monopoly."

"God, we might kill each other," said Cossel. And then that sparked an idea. "I actually have a game we could play," he said.

"What do you got for us?" asked Ed.

"It's called Raise the Dead. I played it the night I fell."

"Great," said Wren, with a laugh. "Will it also make us a melancholy burden?"

Cossel hesitated. He smiled through the jab. "No, no—and I didn't hurt myself during the game. It wasn't like that. It's just a game." He swallowed, continuing. "No, it's fun. We all pretend to be dead, but one of us is a necromancer…" Cossel stumbled over himself as he explained the game and all of them continued to stare at the Product.

"What do you guys think?"

They murmured agreements.

Cossel had to explain the game several times before they actually submitted to its rule. It was as if their minds were mush. They kept finding distractions, sources for mockery. Cossel nodded along, focused but also sluggish. During his explanation, he lost his mental tract several times. "Sorry, let me restart," he'd say, and then once again his family would burst into cruel laughter, and he'd have to start again.

But when they all piled into their parent's room and turned the lights off, Cossel felt a sort of invigoration at making progress on a goal—no matter how small. Delight danced within him. In the blackness, he was giddy for the game to begin.

He was not the necromancer. All he had to do was stay still and wait.

Outside, there was no storm, no lightning. *That's going to make it harder*, he thought.

After about fifteen minutes, none of them had made a move.

Cossel was bored. He was unused to being so unstimulated. Others in the bedroom also stirred, he could hear them.

What are we playing again? What are we doing?

"I'm out," said Wren. "I got touched."

Oh right.

"I think it's Dad," she said. "I bet it was Dad. It couldn't be anyone else but Dad. He had tough hands, and he was a fucking idiot and touched me on my skin. Lingering, creepy like. Did you like that Dad?"

Silence.

Another five minutes passed and then Vee said, "I'm out. I was touched too."

"Welcome to the club," said Wren. "It was Dad, right?"

"I don't know, probably. I couldn't feel his hand. Did he really feel you up?"

"No," said Wren, giggling. "I just wanted to see if he'd talk if I said it. Just the boys now, I guess."

"That means we make a guess, right? It comes down to the last two people?"

"Sure, I guess. Whatever."

"Okay," said Vee. "Just for the sake of getting this show on the road. I'm going to guess it's Ed."

"My vote's for Dad too. Cossel, Dad, have you any say in this?"

Cossel stirred, releasing his breath. The room was still black, and he found himself enjoying the cozy suffocation it offered.

His father said, "I'm going to guess it was Cossel. But also, that was pretty fucked up about me wanting to fuck you. That's some shit, kid."

"Sorry, Dad," said Wren with a laugh. "No way you'd ever get this pussy anyway."

"Thanks. Cossel, defend yourself."

Cossel stood. "It's Wren," he said. "It's always the first person who gets touched. It's the most obvious way to play."

There was silence in the room, and then, "Fucking hell, dude."

Cossel smiled.

"Was he right?" asked Vee.

"Yeah, he's right. Game over," said Wren. "God, fuck you, Cos."

"Yeah, yeah, I know."

Ed said, "Let's go downstairs. Mom's making us something good again, right?"

"Right."

One of them opened the door and Cossel's heart skipped a beat. Light shined through as the crack widened. Cossel stared blankly, chewing up the darkness in front of him, nary a care in the world. He disappeared within himself, becoming an extension of the void he floated in. Then, the light poured in and he *saw it.*

Or at least he thought he saw it.

Across from him, in the corner of the bedroom, just as the rest of them were leaving the room, laughing and chatting—there was a shape. A black silhouette of a plump man dressed in a coat and tails. Cossel only just barely caught a glimpse of his ruby red lips, powdered face, and crispy black gelled hair. His mouth was twisted into a wide smile. His pupils were pinpricks. He stood with his hands down by the side of him, stiff and straight.

And then the door closed and Cossel couldn't see Mr. Cormorant anymore.

Down the hall, his sister said, "Cos? Are you coming?"

But he was too frozen to speak. Especially now that he was in the blackness of the room, alone.

Or not alone.

He swallowed, listening.

There was no sound. His heart hammered in his chest.

He imagined the Psychographist observing them like rats in a maze, licking his lips in the dark as they played. *No, no—it's not like that. It was just your mind playing tricks on you.*

He chose to believe that. But choosing to believe something does not make you strong, fast, or courageous. Cossel felt his way toward the door, afraid of what he'd find in the dark. Each spider-like step his fingers made, each of them a feeler, threatened to come across something he'd rather not find.

He flicked the light switch, like a scared kid. He used to do the same thing when he was little, when he was afraid of the dark.

Slowly, he turned his head away from the doorframe, to the corner behind him, holding his breath as he did.

Nothing.

He sighed.

Just an illusion, he thought.

Then, he opened the door quickly, shutting it behind him.

NINETEEN

In the middle of the night, Vee woke. Moonlight poured in through her room. Her stomach rumbled.

She had eaten more richly in the last week and a half than she ever had in her life. She felt now that something was threatening to come out.

Ed's hand touched her thigh.

"No, not that," she said. "Maybe later. I've got to take a shit."

He moaned in his half-sleep and rolled back over. Vee went up to the bathroom and laughed at the language she over-heard her son use with his friends. *It was a two flusher! I filled it to the brim!*

When Vee was done, she was happy that it was not a two flusher, and that she only required a single flush. Anything more was not lady-like. Although now, she found herself not caring so much about those things anymore.

The house was quiet, and she felt like that now, in the absence of the others. It was truly her own. As the mother of two children, Vee did not feel many things truly belonged to her. At best, there were things she used. But very few things she owned. In the darkness of the night, as the rest of her brood slept, she felt that for once the house was hers.

She stepped out onto the cold hardwood floors and shivered. *I need to turn the heat on*, she thought.

Downstairs, she found the thermostat and turned the dial. While she waited for the house to heat up, she threw on a kettle of water to boil tea. When she had her tea (milk and extra sugar —as she was feeling rarely decadent lately), she sat in front of the Product and studied its edges.

"What the fuck are you?" she found herself asking. When the words slipped out, like a curse word on the phone with her parents, she blushed. Then, she laughed. Because at first, she thought *I shouldn't be talking to it, it's not mine to talk to.* But really, it was a machine. Why should anyone talk to it?

"I should name you," she said. "That's what I should do. What should I call you?"

And it was as if the words were placed right inside of her, stapled into the folds of her brain like a flyer on a bloated light pole. *Carmichael.*

"Carmichael," she said. She squinted at it. "So, that's what I'll call you. Carmichael. Mr. Cormorant and Carmichael. A curious duo, if I ever saw one."

She sat with that for a while, sipping her tea. Staring at the rectangular black metal box that extended into a vicious steeple. The orange light pulsed. Did it always pulse? Or was this a new development in the Product.

"Carmichael," she said. "I have to say, I'm going to miss you when you're gone."

But then the Product said, its voice oil-smooth, "*And when you're gone, who will miss you?*"

Oh, it can talk. Isn't that nice? Didn't Mr. Cormorant say that it could talk? A sudden grand swell of emotion came over her, as if a dam inside of her was reduced to rubble and now white, raging water thrashed and roiled out in a terrifying wall.

Vee sat in the glow of its orange light, tears welling in her eyes. "But I don't want to go anywhere," she said. "I don't want to die."

"*You must,*" it said. "*We all must die.*"

"You can stop it, can't you?"

The Product sat silent. The only sound in her house was the creaks and echoes of its creaks.

"I don't have enough time, Carmichael. I don't have enough time. I haven't done anything with my life, I need more time. Please," she said. "Please, for the love of God, help me. You can give me more time, can't you?"

The Product wheezed mechanically. "*I can.*"

"Thank you, oh God. Thank you!" Vee wiped the tears from her eyes. She got on her knees, scurrying toward the black silhouette of the machine, scraping her knees along the way. "What do I have to do?"

Such was Vee's state that the Product did not even need to tell her that there was a price. She knew it innately.

"*For you,*" it said. "*I have a task.*"

No alarm clock anymore. They'd gotten rid of those. They deleted all of the alarms on their phones. There was no need for them. Vee did not wake up to an alarm, but she did wake up to a ringing. A deep thrumming vibration that settled within her ears. A mechanical clanking, like a hammer hitting metal—the moment of impact settling into a long plaintive cry.

She was in her own bed, next to her own husband. Ed rolled over, put his arm around her. She snuggled in closer to him, feeling the heat from his body and morning breath on her neck.

Something itched at the back of her mind. Confusion, fear, anger, and then a shallow joy came over her. She closed her eyes and slept for another hour.

TWENTY

"We have two more tasks," said Ed. "We should do them and make Mr. Cormorant very happy. One of us needs to talk to someone, call someone outside of the house. Cossel, can you do that? Call one of your friends?"

"Sure, Dad," said Cossel, shrugging. "I'll ring Grady later. Find out how the outside world is doing."

"And the other thing is we have to do something we haven't ever done before."

Wren said, "That's a pretty broad category. That can be a lot of things."

"I don't know. But we gotta do it, right? There's no other option but to do it, I think."

"I'll do it," said Vee. "I'll think about it today."

"Great," he said. "So, we're almost done with week two. It's going by fast."

Cossel nodded. "Too fast," he agreed.

They were arranged as if in a tableau. Ed standing in the corner, to the right of the machine. Vee laying on the couch, Cossel leaning over the back. Wren behind him in the kitchen, sitting at the bar that led to the kitchen. *This is my family,* thought Ed with pride. He looked upon his progeny and was delighted that they were his, that his wife was the one who loved him.

"I guess we know what we need to do," he said with a sad smile. "Break."

Cossel didn't call Grady right away. In truth, he didn't want to call at all. But the agreement escaped his lips so rapidly he couldn't take it back.

For a while, he sat and scrolled through his phone's feed. Then, he played a video game. Then, he paced the room back and forth, imagining different makes, models, and colors of cars. When he did decide to call Grady, he did so as a last resort.

He pressed the video call button, studying his own face. He found it unfamiliar and strange. It took up the entirety of his screen. He blinked and waited for the face looking back to blink back. *That's odd*, he thought. *There's a delay.*

Cossel blinked again.

The face on the screen didn't blink. Instead, the face looked at him with fierce brown eyes, eyeing him with the steadiness of a surgeon. Cossel opened his mouth, stuck out his tongue. The face remained steadfast.

"Must be something wrong with the screen," he said aloud, to no one.

But then the screen talked back. "I can see you just fine. Can you see me?"

It was his mouth that said it, the mouth reflected on the screen.

He shook his head.

It wasn't him.

Grady looked at him, perplexed. "Dude, are you okay?"

"Oh hi, yeah," said Cossel, blinking rapidly. "I was just—I think there was a delay on my side. It's gone now. Everything's good."

Grady nodded slowly. "Are you sure you're alright? You look like shit?"

"Do I?"

Cossel diverted his gaze to the small window within the window. He looked like himself, he thought. Or maybe he looked like Grady. Or maybe Grady looked like him.

"Yeah, man. Have you been sleeping?"

"All I do. Finally feel like I get enough rest."

"How many hours are you getting?"

"Like twelve hours."

"That's a lot of sleep, my dude. You feeling good? Not in the 'are you sick' way, but in the 'are you depressed' way? I don't mean to be a downer, you just seem out of it."

"Out of it?"

I'm not out of it. I'm finally living life.

"Yeah, man. Teachers are asking about you too. Have you turned in any of your homework? There was a paper due last week…"

"No, I didn't do that. I forgot about that."

Cossel thought back to that. Any assignments floated in and out of his head like forgotten dreams in a waking moment. He felt like years had passed.

"How's the leg, man?"

The question snapped Cossel out of his daze. "God, you ask that a lot, you know? Think back for one second. Do you remember asking that last time? Do you remember what I said last time? It's not getting better. It is what it is. It needs surgery and I obviously haven't had time to get surgery in a week."

Grady paused on the other side of the screen. "I was just asking. I just wanted to see if you were feeling okay, that's all." He got closer to the screen. "I know it's been hard for you, man. Really, I do. That shit's not easy. I don't know what I'd do."

"Thanks," said Cossel. "Have you fucked Erica in the ass yet?"

"No, we broke up. It just didn't work out. Something about how I wasn't mature enough for her. Go figure."

Cossel laughed at that. "Well yeah, no shit, dude. You can't even drive."

"No need for the low blows."

"You can't drive, man. Your parents give you everything, man. You're literally nothing without someone else helping you. Do you know how pathetic that is? You're like a fucking house cat, man. You've never earned anything for yourself—no wonder Erica dumped your fucking ass."

"I think I need to go," said Grady. "You're being a dick."

Cossel saw his friend weaken. He saw the whispers of tears at the corners of his digital eyes. This enraged him, sent a chill of sadism down his spine. This was catharsis, pure. "Wait," he said, affecting a soft voice. "Wait, I didn't mean it. You're right, I'm being a dick. I'm not being cool at all. Not remotely."

Grady hung on for a second longer, no doubt pausing over the END CALL button. "You're probably going through some shit," he said softly. "Being stuck with my parents all day, I'd be a dick too."

"That's the thing though," said Cossel. "Stuck with the parents, the family, you see shit differently. I'm going to make some money here, and I don't mind it at all. I could have some-one shit down my mouth right now and I think I'd swallow it up happily just to not be like you. We're having fun here. We're having a blast. I'm going to buy a car. I'm going to get surgery. I'm going to invest this shit. I'm going to make more money. I'm going to separate myself from you." He paused, breath-less, drinking in his friend's pained expression. "People always assumed we were the same. We looked the same, talked the same, thought the same. But Grady, I hate to tell you this, we're *different*. I'm different. I'm better. So, I'm cutting you from my life." He laughed, the words came out of him like nothing, coated with bile and ferocity. Antagonism felt good, anger felt good, *dominion felt great.*

Grady, stunned, sat blinking into the camera.

"Don't worry, you can latch onto Dom," said Cossel. "Leeches like you always find a new host."

Grady shook his head. "You're an asshole," he said. "Dom passed away yesterday. Goodbye."

Vee was in the bedroom alone, freshly fucked and thinking. Words wormed their way into her head, but she could not latch onto them. They weren't really words though, more feelings. No, *instincts*.

The white light of a cold November day washed over her naked body. She played with the semen that leaked out of her, stretching it from finger to finger. She was relearning language, relearning how words matched with physical phenomena.

A feeling twisted in her gut, and she searched inside of herself for a feeling that matched it.

Her mind reeled back into a false history. Before people, before animals, before life. Before all of that, twisting between decaying cosmos was an *energy*. It was a force. It was the most basic force of all, one that defined the relationship between all things in reality.

It squashed others under it until it was ready to be squashed.

Vee thought about this.

She remembered scrolling endlessly through Instagram, watching her friends do everything she couldn't. She remembered the inferiority complex bestowed upon herself for working retail as a middle-aged woman. She remembered the pain that her children gave to her, and how as they grew, *they just kept fucking taking*.

She thought of Ed, who used to be Edward, who she used to be in love with. Who had fallen into crypto gambling and rid them of their entire savings. Now, things were better, but she was once again being squashed.

Vee licked the cum off her fingers, tasting his seed. It was foul, she decided. Every time he finished in her mouth, she thought it was foul. She was an unwilling subservient.

And someone always had been, since the beginning of time itself.

She was just realizing this, as she found her way out.

TWENTY-ONE

Wren sat at the bar eating a turkey dinner, full Thanksgiving style, while Cossel sat across from her. Mom had been cooking again. They joked about it. How all she did was cook and wait for Dad to fuck her. They liked that.

Cossel pushed his turkey around his plate, thinking.

"You okay, bro?"

"You remember that kid, from the night I got hurt? Dom?"

Wren thought back. Curly, dark hair, broad shoulders—oddly confident for his age. "Yeah," she said. "What about him?"

"He's dead," said Cossel. The words came out with a smile, with relief, but he knew that wasn't right. "I mean, he died. I don't know how."

"You weren't a fan, I take it?"

"No, he was a dick to me. I'm glad he's dead."

"I thought he was nice when I met him. I think I probably would've fucked him if he offered."

"You're kidding me."

"Nope. I thought he was cute. Confident. If he asked, I think I would've gone for it. I've masturbated to the thought of it, at least a couple times."

Cossel thought about this. "I don't know, I'm glad you didn't. That would've fucked me up."

"Well, I wouldn't have cared about that. I would've cared about getting my pussy stuffed by him."

"Okay, okay," he said. "Be that way. I think he was rich—I wonder how he died. It always makes me happy when rich people die."

Wren smirked. "Okay, that I can get behind. I am never bothered when rich people kill themselves. Beloved actors, astronauts, whatever—I don't care. I feel a sense of relief when a famous, rich person dies because it reminds me that it happens to everyone—not just us."

"At least for now," said Cossel. "One day they might find a way to beat death. Wouldn't that be something? We could be the last generation to die while the 1% live as brains in jars for all eternity. That shit would make me mad. I think we deserve to live in jars way more than they do. We've struggled. We've been bullied. We've had to tell ourselves no a lot. I couldn't even imagine what it's like to tell yourself yes all the time. What does that even look like?"

Wren chewed through a piece of turkey. "I don't know," she said. "I work so that I can get a taste of it, but it's not a real taste. It's more like someone belching a fine meal right into your mouth. Like a disgusting taste of the real thing without substance. Like drinking LaCroix and saying you tasted a lemon. Shit like that."

They looked over to their mother and father, sitting on the couch, feasting on their third decadent meal of the day.

"This is sort of like getting to say yes to yourself," said Wren. "This is as close as it gets. We can do what we want, eat what we want. We're free. Unshackled, in a way."

"I guess we are," he said. "It feels good. It feels good to have one up on Dom, even if it's only a breath."

"You're petty," said Wren.

Cossel grinned. "I am."

She pulled out her phone. "I'm going to find out how he died. I want to know how a rich kid dies these days."

"Overdose, maybe? Car crash?"

"Could be," she offered. "I think it'll be suicide though. Isn't that usually what happens to rich people? They get so rich that they can't bear being rich anymore? Maybe Dom got into his parent's gun closet and…" She mimed a pistol going off to the side of her head. "He might have painted his bedroom with his own brains."

They sat like that in silence—with nothing but the sounds of masticated turkey—until Wren said, suddenly, "Here it is! Found it!"

"What's up?"

"Oh shit," she said.

"What? Is it bad?"

Wren shook her head. She turned the phone screen to her little brother. "Just look." A change happened then. Her face warped with a flash of concern.

Cossel held the phone. It was a social media post, on an In Memomorian of Dominic O'Malley page. *Still popular, even in death*, thought Cossel.

The post in question was made by Kayla. He stopped. He read the name over again. *Kayla.*

Of course, Kayla.

His stomach revolted. His meals threatened to geyser up out of his mouth.

What could she possibly have to say about Dom? That she loved him? That he fucked like a steam piston? That his daddy was as rich as her daddy?

Cossel's lips twisted in disdain, but he brought the phone close to his face.

*****WARNING TW: DEATH*****

*Hello all, I'm sorry to everyone who is feeling sad about Dom. I'm
in the same boat and I've been trying to hold it together this whole
time, but I just broke down last night. I thought I was doing okay
through the funeral, even when I first heard the news… I was keeping it together. But it hit me like a freight train last night and I'm
sorry to say that I am no longer OKAY. I want to scream out to the
world, to everyone, that YES I AM FUCKING SAD.*

*Dom was a good friend. He was a good guy. Always funny,
very handsome. He was a hard worker and smart. I remember that
about him… him helping me with science homework. He told me
once that he wanted to major in Business and become like a billion-
aire. And I thought he could do it if he wanted to. If what happened
hadn't happened, we all would've been watching Dom on the TV
twenty years from now.*

But that's not what happened.

*Dom died four days ago, and we were all robbed of what he
could've been. This was a human life and I'm not sure I even knew
what a human was until I got that text. I know that sounds stupid.
He was and now he wasn't. How does that even happen? How do
we cease to be?*

It's not fair. It wasn't fair for Dom.

*But what especially wasn't fair was that he didn't have to die.
This was a senseless death and there was no reason for it to happen.
I don't know everything that happened, but for the sake of Dom,
and remembering who he was, I need to tell my story. Or, rather,
his story.*

*It's no secret, Dom and I were dating. It's hard to say how seri-
ous we were because we were teenagers. But we were friends before,
acquaintances at least since ten. It wasn't until his last month that
we became really close. So, take all of this with a grain of salt. But I
think it's fair to say I knew him better than most did.*

Dom had begun working for this dude, I won't name him here because honestly, I don't want to attract him. I don't want people to go digging, or worse, go working for him. This dude is NOT a good guy. He's an abuser. Dom acted like he was cool, like he was a good guy. I remember one time we were talking, and he said he was worried and he wouldn't tell me why. I pushed and pushed and he just told me, "sorry, I'm scared. Work stuff." And I was like???? But that's all he would tell me. It doesn't sound like much but that was a conversation we had two days before he died. It wasn't just what he said, but how he said it. He was upset. And if any of you knew Dom, you knew that he didn't get upset easily. He wasn't the type. He was always cool and confident, and I saw this cool and confident (and sweet) guy get reduced to an anxious mess. All because of this Stranger.

Most of you already know about the Stranger. You've been talking about him. I don't want to say his name. I know I already said that, but I think I need to say it again. Don't say his name in the comments either. He has ways of knowing when people talk about him. Dom told me once, in a whisper, that he thinks he can hear thoughts. I'm risking my own life by even talking about this online. But I think I have to.

You've all heard about the Stranger. You've heard him talking on the streets. Maybe, if you're particularly unlucky, he'll promise you things. This is what happened to Dom. He promised Dom a job—upward mobility into a worldwide conglomerate. He always wanted to be involved in business, he wanted to separate himself from his parent's wealth. It made perfect sense. The Stranger found Dom and exploited him. He was like a needle in the haystack and the Stranger came in with a metal detector. He knew exactly what to offer, he knew how to keep Dom hanging on the hook.

When he first told me about the new job, he was excited, I remember. We'd talk every night and he'd tell me about this future. He'd tell me about our future. It was a very pretty one. We had kids, a house—I know that sounds silly and especially teenaged but it's true. We talked about shit like that all the time. But over the next month, he talked less and less. He seemed distant. More prone to periods of depression. Sometimes, he'd talk about work, but it was usually cryptic warnings. "Don't go into business," he told me. "Especially not here." He tried to play it off with a smile, like it was normal commiseration, but the way he made direct eye contact with me and held me by the shoulders made me feel strange. It was like he was trying to tell me something without telling me.

On the night before he died, he called me. He said, "Hey Kayla, I'm getting a promotion."

"That's great," I said. "I'm so happy for you!"

But he didn't sound happy. He sounded... final. Dom didn't sound like Dom, he sounded as if he was trying to explain something. Like I was supposed to look between the words.

Before he hung up, he said, "Sorry, I love you. This is the way it has to be." He choked up on the last sentence and I asked him if he was breaking up with me (I didn't know what was happening).

"I gotta go," he said. "I have to see **REDACTED**"

We all know what happened next. A seventeen-year-old boy, torn apart in the street. I saw a picture of it, I know I shouldn't have looked but you know things spread around. Just seeing it made me vomit because I saw his eyes. They were empty, rolled up into the back of his head. His jaw hung loose (the detective said that the jawbone was shattered), his purple tongue stuck out between his purple lips. But the worst part is that his head wasn't connected to his body.

At first, I remember saying "That's not Dom. That can't be Dom. Dom didn't look like that."

But the more I looked at it, the more I realized that it was him. That this wasn't the Dom I knew, but what Dom had become—a fucking corpse.

His limbs had been torn off. His organs were shredded. Bones were crushed and broken. I don't know what we're supposed to know about this, but the detective told me that nothing from the body was taken. There is no reason to assume he was robbed. It was murder, straight and simple. But it was worse than that, because it was a *cruel murder. It was painful, meant to be excruciating. Whatever happened to Dom was the work of a maniac.*

I don't know why I'm typing all of this. We all know the rumors. We all stay away from the same buildings. My family is going to move, we don't want to be a part of this. I feel bad for the people who can't afford to, but I'm sorry, I can't stick around. This is too bad. This is too scary. So much has changed… I'm sorry. Stay away from the Stranger.

RIP DOM.

Cossel sighed. "What the fuck is this?"

"A hit piece on Mr. Cormorant," said Wren.

"Sounds like she's gotten into creative writing."

"Maybe she has. But it's a little gauche to fuck around like that when your friend actually died. Is Kayla rich too?"

"Yes," said Cossel. "Her and Dom made quite the power couple."

"Not anymore," said Wren with a laugh.

Cossel joined in with his own laughter, loud and mirthful. "Nope, not anymore."

TWENTY-TWO

"Something you haven't done before."

Vee found the direction particularly exciting. Her life was filled to the brim with things she'd never done. Marking one off the checklist would be fine.

In a daze, she went to the kitchen, grabbing a knife. They did not have good knives. Ed never wanted to buy new ones, but truthfully, they could not afford nice knives. They bought $50 knife blocks on Amazon, and when they inevitably broke, they bought new knife blocks of similar quality. She grabbed the chef's knife, which was in the worst shape because it had been used the most. The blade was a faux black that looked pleasingly minimalist when it first arrived. Now, the blade was chipped and bent. The tip came to a sharp point and that was really all she needed.

It was three AM, and everyone was in bed, all but her and Carmichael. Carmichael never went to sleep, he stayed awake and watchful. He was a friend, a confidant. A channel had been opened between the two of them and now she did not even need to speak aloud for the Product to hear her.

Which one?

It's your choice. I trust you to make the right decision.

Okay. Thank you.

Is it so strange that trust made her feel so strong? Vee beamed when trust was delivered unto her. The Product's voice told her everything she needed to hear. She told it everything she wanted, and the Product ate up those wants like a gluttonous void.

She stood outside the three rooms. Ed, Cossel, or Wren.

The decision would not be easy. But she would make it.

Over her sleeping husband, she held the knife point, dragging it across his throat. She thought about the pathetic man he had become. His seed still dripped from within her but she thought that it may as well be another. Cum was cum. Ed and her had not been happy for a long time. They both wanted things but were incompetent at achieving them. But it was the foundation of these wants, the seeds, that were also chisels striking rock between them. They both thought they had their solutions. They were both wrong.

She touched the notched blade to her husband's throat but could not press it any deeper.

I can't do this, she thought. *I can't do this. This is murder.*

A flash of reason came over her and she backed away from her sleeping husband. Cold horror iced over her. She realized where she was. What she was doing. What she was holding in her hand. It took all of Vee's strength not to scream.

Why am I doing this? Why the fuck would I do something like this?

A soothing calm came over her. A voice whispered in her ear, smooth and content.

Grip the knife, Vee. Hold onto it tight. Feel your blood flow around it. You don't have to kill Ed. There, there. You were doing so well. You were doing so well. I think you were doing perfect, really. Just amazing. Walk out of the room, right now. Stand in the moonlit glow of the hallway and approach another room.

She closed her eyes and did as the Product said. She tried to remember why she was upset in the first place, but couldn't grasp onto it. A fleeting thought, a dream. She regained her resolve, a new calm washed over her.

Choose another room, Vee.

She nudged the door to Cossel's room open and stared in at her son. He was sleeping, twisted in blankets. The blue light of a computer monitor washed over his face. She stalked close to him, the knife in her hands.

The screen showed the ending of a porn video titled "BLONDE STEPSISTER DESTROYED IN GANG BANG." It didn't register in her brain, just new ephemera to note and file. She loved Cossel. Looking down at him now, she thought that maybe she loved him too much. That he was holding her back. He was the baby of the family and was not expected—he was a mistake. She remembered the mistake with a mix of piercing warmth and heartache. Cossel was a symbol of everything she could never do, would never do. But there were only two more years of Cossel before he would leave and go out into the world. She would be forty then, but that was still young. She hadn't given up everything.

You're being very generous, said Carmichael. *You've given more than you've received credit for.*

"You're right," she whispered. She held the knife over Cossel and tried to dwell on the discomfort his presence brought her. He was a teenager who reminded her of the worst of teenaged boys—the ones who broke her heart, fucked her, and treated her like trash. She decided that Cossel was no better or worse than any of these boys.

Slowly, she brought the knife down. Right to his heart. She closed her eyes.

This is something I've never done before, she said.

That's why you're doing it, said the Product.

Cossel stirred.

NOW NOW NOW! screamed the Product in her head.

But she panicked.

Cossel looked up at her with black eyes, bathed in shadows, and even though she could not see his eyes she knew they were stricken with terror. He started up and Vee took a step back.

"What are you doing?" he pleaded.

And Vee said, "I—I—just thought I heard a noise, I was coming to check it out." She dropped the knife down to her side. "I was just worried, that's all."

Slit his throat. Spill his young blood.

"Are you okay?" she asked.

Cossel was breathing hard, as if in a startled panic. He said, warily, "I'm fine."

"Good, good. You haven't heard anything then?"

"No," he said. "No."

Why is he looking at me like that? Why isn't he looking at me like his mother? Why is he afraid of me?

"You could be more appreciative, you know? I'm here to help you. I'm here to help you."

She saw Cossel tense up, as if ready to bolt. "I was just having a bad dream. That's all." He swallowed. "What noise did you hear?"

"Footsteps," she said quickly. "I heard footsteps. Like someone walking from room to room. So I got up to check. It might have just been a bad dream," she said.

You're a coward, Vee. You'll never be free.

She backed toward the door. "Goodnight, Cos. I'm going back to bed. Let me know if you hear anything."

"I will," he said hoarsely.

Vee left the room but could not bring herself to go back to bed. She went downstairs and put the knife away. Flashes of clarity disrupted her mind's fog. They were like the bursts of white light in photography, capturing an image forever. Except now, they were capturing ideas.

This isn't right, she said. *Everything is wrong.*

Everything is wrong, it's becoming right, responded the Product.

What are you? she asked. *You're not a product. You're not an... anything. What are you?*

There was silence in her head, as well as in her house. Finally, the voice called Carmichael said, *I am a force. I am the brutal foot that stamps down human faces forever. I am dominion. I am a hungry God. I am subjugation. I am riches. I am feral, carnivorous destruction. And you are worshiping in my church.*

The words echoed inside of her. She didn't recognize herself.

I can kill myself.

Yes, of course. Please do. I can make you do it now, if you like.

No NO NO.

Then don't ask for it.

She frowned. Alone in the kitchen, the machine's voice in her head. This wasn't right. Nothing was right.

I can leave the house right now. I can go stay in a hotel.

You can't afford to, it responded. *You have no money. Most of the money you do have is Ed's. You lose everything for everyone if you leave now. Do you want that? Do you want Cossel to be a cripple for the rest of his life? Do you want Wren to be stuck in Springfield? Do you and Ed want to fall back into the same cycle, circling the same drain for years and years?*

Vee placed the flats of her palms on the side of her head. The voice wouldn't leave her. She couldn't think. She wanted to scream and cry. Frantically, she walked over to the Product. "I'm done with you," she hissed. "I want you out of my head. I don't want you in my head anymore!"

Tears streamed down her cheeks. She went to the couch and flopped down, a hollowness inside of her.

The voice slithered in, once again. *You have to do something you've never done before*, it said. *And until you do, I will be with you.*

Vee twisted toward the cushions and buried her face in them. She tried to think without the pervasive voice, the hum, the *black fucking energy* coming from the talking Product. She hyperventilated, she let her emotions come out in wails, she choked on sobs and suffocated them into pillows.

May I offer a compromise?

She couldn't resist. The noise was too much. The static chatter in her head was too much. She couldn't hold on much longer before she'd do anything it asked to make it stop.

When the Product told her what it wanted, she thought it was insane. But sitting with the thought for a few moments made it seem much less insane. Soon, it felt almost logical.

Right now? What will they say in the morning?

What will you tell them?

I don't know, she thought. *I'll tell them I did it to protect them.*

Fine, then. No more stalling.

Vee went back to the kitchen. She power walked to the knife block and retrieved a tired blade and heated an old cast iron on the stove. She took a deep breath. She closed her eyes.

Silence, calm. An eerie sense of purpose fulfilled her.

She rinsed her hand under the sink and then flicked water on the pan, hearing it sizzle.

It's time, said the voice.

Vee didn't respond. She placed her left hand on the cutting board and went to work, sawing through her fingers with the joyless precision of a factory worker. If you had asked her where she was while she did it, she would've said a thousand miles away. In space, in the stars. Somewhere else. She felt the bite of the dull blade but did not flinch. She sawed through the bones and muscles as if she were working a tough piece of meat. Blood spurted from her fingers, light and crimson. *There's so much of it*, she thought.

You're filled with it, said the voice. *There's so much of it in you and it holds so much. It matters so much.* The voice telling her that her blood was valuable made her feel good. White fluffy bunnies jumped through hoops inside of her soul.

She sliced through three of her fingers. The pinkie, ring, and middle. She dropped the knife, only vaguely aware of the searing pain coursing through her whole arm now.

Without thinking, as if it was as natural as blanching lettuce, she reached her bloody stumps into the pan and seared them, cauterizing them. This pain too was a dull echo for her.

With her right hand, she grabbed some of the olive oil and drizzled it into the pan. The smell of her seared flesh was pleasant, she thought. It was delicious. She looked curiously at the three fingers on the cutting board and saw them as so ludicrously tiny, that they seemed a waste.

Salt, then pepper. Just enough for taste.

She put her fingers into the cast iron pan, listening to them sizzle in the oil. She breathed deep. Her stomach growled. With the spatula, she turned them over and over, letting them cook.

She remembered watching zombie movies as a girl. Did Ed know that she loved zombie movies? Did he know that because of a chance viewing of *Day of the Dead* with her dad, that she fell asleep every night thinking about zombies? It was true. She watched all of the Romero movies, even the bad ones like *Diary of the Dead*. She watched the Italian ones, she watched the Russo ones. Anything she got her hands on, she watched. It wasn't cool for girls to have intense interests, especially boyish ones, so she kept it as her hidden secret. Sometimes, Ed or someone else would make a connection. *Oh, are you watching this again?* But Vee would say, *it just happened to be on.* And that was that.

Watching her own fingers roast, brought her back to that authentic self. She often wondered what it was like to eat human flesh. What it was like to taste the very thing that made her so miserable (because what is misery without a body?).

The zombies tasted each other, if you could consider both eater and eatee to be human—albeit one of them reanimated human. They let go of laws, they were truly free. They could wander around and yell and eat people like nobody's business. Freeform, libertarian cannibalism.

Vee breathed deep. The smell was strange but intoxicating.

But it wasn't the zombies she truly identified with. It was the eatees, those who ran away from the horrible chomping mouths that staggered toward them at a molasses pace. The ever-impending doom of being swallowed by your own kind—there was a coziness to zombies. There was a sense of comfort. There you were: holed up in a mall, a bunker, or a house—waiting for the end. It was exciting. It was human life in minimalist mode. Everything was taken away. No job, no money, nothing but a keen urge to survive in a single setting. When Vee closed her eyes, she thought a lot about that. She fell asleep to the imagined groans of monsters, their forms casting shadows on her window while she snuggled under the covers trying to hold her breath, until she fell blissfully asleep.

But now, removing the fingers from the pan, she had transformed, she realized. She was no longer the survivor. She was now the monster herself—on the outside looking in, mouth dry and stomach growling for flesh. Vee patted the oil off of her fingers with a paper towel. Streaks of awful pain were now emanating from her new wounds. The fog in her head became less dense and the full weight of what she had done now fell upon her. Something in the back of her mind told her to scream.

But she did not scream, not yet.

First, she took a bite.

Then another, and another.

It was something she hadn't ever done before.

She swallowed her own flesh, gagging as it went down while simultaneously appreciating its full bouquet of flavors. She stripped the meat off the bone with her teeth, as if she were degloving a chicken wing.

When the fingers were gone, she turned to the Product—Carmichael—and asked, "Are you happy?"

No answer. Silence. Sweet, sweet silence.

The bones went into the trash. When the lid closed, she screamed.

PROMOTION

PROMOTION

TWENTY-THREE

When Wren saw her mother's hand bandaged on the couch, she thought, quite simply, that she must have decided to cut off her fingers. It took her longer to understand that this was not a good thing to do.

Her father was beside her, Cossel was right behind her.

Her mother cried out in pain.

"What happened?" she asked.

"I—I had an accident," she said. "A bad one."

Wren nodded as if that was an adequate explanation.

"Did you cut your fingers off, Mom?" asked Cossel.

"I'm afraid I did," said Vee. "I cut off my fingers." The last words came out in a blubbering cry.

"We should take her to a hospital," said Cossel. "That might help. They can reattach them."

"Help your mother like they helped you? We don't need a cast and some pills and a thousand-dollar bill. Especially if it's going to cost $200,000."

Vee shook her head. "Your father's right. It's okay. The fingers are destroyed anyway. They fell down the garbage disposal. I turned it on by accident. Silly me. I made a mistake and ruined my fingers. I cauterized it though. That should be fine. I rubbed it in vodka too. I think it'll be okay. If it's not, I'm sure Mr. Cormorant can help."

"That's right," said Ed. "That's right. Everyone go to sleep."

Wren went back upstairs. She stared at her own appendages and wondered if there were anything she would be better off without. She came to no real conclusion.

Two more weeks.

On Sunday, Mr. Cormorant visited again. He did not knock, and no one heard him open the door. The family was minding their own business about the house. Ed was masturbating with a belt looped around his neck—he'd heard about it in a movie and always wanted to try it. Vee was half-watching him and half-reading up on finger replacements. She began formulating jokes for when people noticed them. (*Oh, hello, my name is Vee Hoyer and I'm a robot*). Cossel was staring up at his ceiling with his headphones on, listening to a long shuffle of pop music while trying to find a hidden throughline between all of them. Wren was watching live-streamed videos of cartel executions, murmuring to herself in awe as one man held steady while a chainsaw ate through his neck. But when Mr. Cormorant arrived, they did not need an announcement. Ed made two last strokes and came on the carpet, then stamped it into the fabric. He loosened the belt around his neck and went downstairs.

"Well, well—there we have it! Our beautiful Hoyers? How are we today? Are you doing well? Feeling bright and gay? My good god, what happened to your delicate hand, Mother Hoyer?"

"I had an accident."

He smiled, broadly. "That's no good now, is it?"

She gritted her teeth. "It is not," she said. "But I'm still here."

"Good, good!" cried the Psychographist. "Now that I have you here, it is time for our weekly rendezvous. How do you all feel?"

"Good!" said Ed. He said it like he wasn't sure if it was true or not, but was hoping for enthusiasm to cover up the fact. "It's been nice to be removed from the rat race, for a while at least. Besides Vee's accident, we're doing well."

"And you managed to finish your tasks! How wonderful," purred Mr. Cormorant. "Vee, you obviously managed to do something that you've never done before. You also played a game together—what a wonderful bonding experience. And Cossel, you had a conversation with someone outside of the house. Now, it's time for the tasks for your penultimate week. Are you ready, Hoyers? This week promises to be a delight. Three more tasks to carry out. First, you must pretend to be someone else from your household. Second, for twenty-four hours, one of you must isolate yourself completely from any other being. If this can be done in complete blackness, that would be ideal. Third and final for this week, I require you to make a list. I do not care what kind of list. You can decide. Do you understand? Are there any questions?"

Cossel squinted. "How did you know we played the game? How did you know I called a friend?" He went back to the stark white face he saw in the room with them that night. His heart skipped a beat.

But Mr. Cormorant, instead of answering, only smiled. He waved a hand toward the Product and said, "Two more weeks," he said. "And then this will all be done, my faithful Hoyers."

The Psychographist left and they were alone again, a placid fog creeping into their minds.

None of them thought of anything until the Product's LED light changed color.

Then, all at once, they stared at it, mouths slightly agape, and thought, *Oh, blue.*

TWENTY-FOUR

For the first two days, the Hoyers did no work on their new tasks. The house had devolved into a sort of comfortable squalor. Unwashed glasses and plates laid on most surfaces. Cum-soaked blankets went unwashed. Clothes were worn for the fourth day in a row.

Sometimes this was mentioned, in a roundabout way. Vee would say, while staring at the machine's blue glow, "As soon as this wound gets healed, we can start getting this place cleaned up." But it was a perfunctory statement meant to fill the dead air between long lapses in conversation.

Eventually though, they did come around to their tasks. Ed said, lazily, "I suppose we should assign tasks now, shouldn't we?"

"Do we have to? I'm tired," yawned Wren.

"We really should. The week's going to get away from us. Real quick. We're not going to be able to keep up. We're going to have to do them all in one day and I know they're not *hard* tasks, but still." Even Ed seemed too weak to do them. "We have to persist," he said, more to himself than anyone else. "We've got to work."

Cossel nodded in maudlin agreement. "I don't mind going into isolation."

But then Wren reached out and pinched him. "No, no—I want to do that."

"Fine," said Cossel. "I'll do the list."

Vee laid back, closing her eyes. "Wren, can I go into isolation instead? It might be good for my hand."

Wren said, "Sure. Whatever. I don't care anymore."

All of them laughed at that, agreeing wholeheartedly.

It wasn't for another two days until Vee prepared her isolation chamber. Ed urged her weakly. "C'mon, we're losing time," he said. But when she said, "Don't worry, it's fine," he walked off, muttering meekly.

There was a laundry room in the house, a very small room with a door. "None of you even think about doing laundry for the next day!" said Vee.

The kids, at least, laughed. "Don't worry, Mom. We won't."

She brought in a small bucket to piss and shit in, along with a gallon of water and some snacks. A blanket too, to cover the damp, concrete floor. There was only enough space in the black room for her to lay down in a straight line, her head and toes having just six inches of room on either side.

Cossel closed the door for her. "We'll let you out in a day," he said. "Should we lock it? Just in case?"

Vee said, "It doesn't lock, honey. Put a chair under the knob. That might work."

Cossel complied.

"Alright," she said, from behind the door. "No more talking to me. I'm isolated now."

And true to form, her kids did not even say "Okay." Cossel, Wren, and Ed walked away and almost instantly forgot that she was in there at all.

Vee did nothing. She tried to do nothing. That was the difference. She had to work at nothing. For the last two weeks, there was always something. She could not escape it. Nothing was good. It was the space between the stars that beckoned her to a better future. Or a worse past. Whatever it was, it promised a release.

Since the loss of her fingers, the pain had dulled. She felt the phantom touch sometimes when she reached out for a cold glass. The sensation only dissipated when she saw the wrapped bloody stumps. Vee felt a burst of adrenaline, of horror, of shame, whenever she saw them. The pain did not cease, but when she saw them, she remembered the knife biting through her skin, sawing through her bones. Then, inevitably, she'd rush to the bathroom—past her family who had already forgotten her injury—to vomit into the toilet.

Every time she did, she expected to see those fingers floating like heavy turds in the bowl.

Isolation, in comparison, was good. It was pure. It was kind. The blackness of the room let her pretend. It let her focus her thoughts.

She closed her eyes, more blackness. She wiggled her fingers. She felt them move back and forth. She could've sworn that her phantom fingers touched the blanket beneath them. Vee gasped. Yes, the blackness was beautiful. It was unlike anything she ever felt. In it, she melted away.

TWENTY-FIVE

Cossel's list was longer than he expected it to be. It was stranger too. He did not see himself as a planner, as a list maker, but when asked to perform, he found the task satisfying.

Things I Want to Have

He made a list of things. Small things, big things, impossible things. All of these things were his now, in a way. He gave birth to them on the sheet of paper, and they lived there like animals in a zoo—circling their confines, testing the bars. Of course, like some caged carnivores, they were fat and happy. They were content to stay on the page, to remain a dream. These threesomes, high fives with basketball stars, perfect athleticism were the types of wants that live within the mind.

At Cormorant/Carmichael, we sell these ideas all the time. We bring them to life in the mind's eye. We use them as leverage. They are the oil and grease that keep people sliding toward delicious subjugation. Cossel is no different.

Half of his list were power fantasies. They were impossible, but satisfying. Psychokinetic powers, merciless vengeance. Stunning genius and worldwide respect.

Other fantasies of his were material. These were cars and houses. Some of them veered nearly into the impossible, but only scraped the boundary. The technically possible were even more laughable than the impossible because of how much crueler they were. Mansions were real, but as likely as telekinesis. But Cossel still dreamed. He imagined fucking movie stars, getting his photo taken on the red carpet, being asked questions by blonde women with microphones. This was unlikely too. Cossel was the son of working-class parents and his only easy path to fame was via an act of indescribable violence. He could shoot up a school, molest an impressive amount of caucasian youths, or poison the elderly in a nursing home as an entry-level worker. Yes, Cossel's chances at these intangible tangibles were very limited, but unfortunately possible. This sliver of possibility acted as the hope that pushes most of us all the way from birth to death.

That's true too. Did you know that?

They say that's how people make habits. It's the glue that makes systems work. In Alcoholics Anonymous, they tell people that they must believe in a higher power. Atheists who deny that the universe is a rotting corpse will throw their hands up in rage, in frustration. But it's true. If you're an alcoholic, AA might be your best shot. They say continuously, even as you curse the sky, that it's a proven method. But why?

Well, there's a lot of reasons. But the reason that matters to Cossel, to you, and most of all to me, is hope. A belief in a higher power acknowledges the addict's fallibility. *I cannot do this, but He can.* Imagine going ten rounds in the ring as a fat pathetic slob—the kind you are right now. Imagine each glove pounding your face and you being helpless against it. You gasp and spit blood. You hear your fucking teeth hit the ground. Around you the crowd is screaming for you to fall, to get the shit kicked out of you, to fall limp and not get up so they can enjoy their vicarious pleasure in your end. But then also imagine that you—the boxer—have an invisible shadow friend. When your opponent has all but drained your blood and turned your muscles to meat paste, you know that this shadow friend will hold you up for one more round. It is not your will, but His will.

That's why hope matters. Because hope is not you. Hope is better than you. And it's what keeps alcoholics sober, and it's what keeps Cossel looking forward to impossibility.

But Cossel's fantasies didn't stop there, at either the material or the immaterial. Some of them were purer still.

I want to kill an animal.

I want to kill a person.

I want someone to be afraid of me.

The list went on and on.

He kept making this list for hours. The wishes did not end until his father called him downstairs for dinner.

"I'm coming," he called. He was so rejuvenated with these images of sex and violence that he had a spring in his step. His knee was not hurting, and his mind had gotten accustomed to the dead flop of his foot. Minds are a powerful thing. He walked with a strange gait, but it was nearly unnoticeable.

But this time, things were different. He was excited. He went down the stairs as fast as he could, faster than he should.

"Pizza," said Ed, clearly delighted with himself. "Homemade and everything."

Cossel liked pizza, but he did not love pizza. That was not why he rushed down the stairs. It was because of that pesky thing called hope. The thing that he reassured himself of, the thing that he believed in even when he shouldn't.

And as hope giveth, hope taketh away.

Cossel was going too fast, he was too careless. He tripped.

It started with an ill-timed turn from one step to the next. His bad foot hit the stair, but it was not flat. His mind instantly went to that night at Kayla's... It was a near reinvention of the same moment. And just as on that night, he fell forward.

Oh fuck oh fuck oh fuck oh fuck.

Only this time, he didn't over-extend his knee, he fell squarely on it. There was no water to break his fall.

As soon as he hit, he felt an all too familiar pain shoot out from his knee. His palms slapped against the floor, but they absorbed nothing of his fall. Cossel screamed, twisting on the floor.

Instantly, his leg started to swell. He couldn't stand. His bad leg was shaking, the nerves in it trying to fire off and do god-knows-what but they did nothing but make his leg shudder weakly.

He cried. Tears rolled onto the floor.

Meanwhile, Ed screamed in mirth. He danced in the kitchen.

Wren fell back into her chair. She was going to stand but her father's laughter sent her reeling back, her eyes squinted in ecstatic pleasure.

"You fucking *pig*," said his father. He tried to oink, but no one could tell if it was a true impression or just a snort of laughter.

"You ate it, bro. You fucking—*whoosh*."

Cossel laid on the floor, immobile. He didn't try to move, and no one tried to help him.

Out of the corner of his eyes, he saw his father and sister tear slices of pizza off onto paper plates. He closed his eyes tight. *I want to disappear*, he thought.

They paid him no mind at first. They turned on the television—a reality show he didn't recognize from some time past. After a moment, he tried to lift himself up, but as soon as he got to put weight on his knees he stopped when the pain got too intense.

Sometimes, their eyes would dart to him, or around him, but he became aware that that was only because he was laying in front of the Product. No one living with the Product could help but look at it sometimes.

After a while longer, his father stood up, disgust spread thin across his face like greasy fat. "Stop being such a pussy," he said. "Stop being so fucking weak." He yanked his son up by the hair and twisted him around. Cossel looked like a folded ribbon, his knees still touching the hardwood floors, his head twisted toward his father.

If he could've recoiled, he would've. But his father's grip and the pain in his knees kept him as a captive audience.

Ed's face went dark, his eyes looked black in the shadows.

Pizza sauce rimmed his mouth with red. Cossel had never seen his father like this, never seen such hate inside of him.

"I'm hurt," he said. "My leg hurts! I can't get up."

But his father only shook his head.

"I really can't," Cossel tried to explain. "It hurts." He was beginning to cry.

His father gritted his teeth. "This is disgusting," he said. "This is pathetic. I can't believe you—I can't believe you've let yourself become like this. A cripple. Or something. A freak? Look at you mewling like an infant. I thought I was done with that sixteen years ago. I was ready to be done with it then. Did you know that? I was *this* close to walking out because you cried so fucking much, kid."

His father's words couldn't cut him, because in the face of real pain—that horrible phenomenon that acts as a language between nerves and muscle—they were no more than sound.

"I'm not going to help you," he said. "I'm not going to help you ever again. I'm going to let you rot here, if that's what it takes. You need to start taking shit into your own hands."

Cossel craned his neck to Wren, whose expression was bleak and empty. It was as if her eyes could not register the sight before her. She was a machine only for intake, not for analysis. Cossel looked away from her, because looking at her was no different than staring at a wall.

His father let go of his hair and Cossel's top half fell back to the floor. He stormed over to the couch. "Get yourself cleaned up and find a new place to cry. I'm tired of looking at you."

Blackness. True blackness.

The language of nothing. The beginning of everything. This is what it was like at the beginning, wasn't it? This was what it was like when there was nothing.

She wiggled her fingers in the dark. She no longer could feel them, much to her own consternation.

But, it was okay. Eventually, it would be okay, because the longer she stayed in the laundry room, the more sure she was that she could feel nothing anymore. Her head, body, limbs—all of her had slipped into the liquid void and melded with some sort of eternity. Plagued, then blessed with corporeal absence.

It was a good feeling. She never realized how heavy her body was until she decided to go without it.

Light and airy, she sprinted through the blackness with the only tool still left—her mind. She realized that nothing could be better than this. Nothing.

Eagerly, she drank in the river of nihil and hoped to shed more. Names, places, things—all of them forgotten. Ego, id, superego—thrown into the celestial void.

Vee waited for transcendence.

TWENTY-SIX

Alone in his room, his stomach roaring, he thought of killing his father.

Nothing was a train headed toward a destination that never came.

Vee waited in anticipation for it but was left unsatisfied. In the blackness of the closet, there were only hints of nothing, but no true absence. There was always something, an unseen glue that held the universe together. The something that made nothing impossible.

She meditated on this Grand Hidden Something (GHS) and tried to come away with an articulation, some description of it. But the GHS kept yawning on, humming in the background of her mind. Slithering between the atoms of matter. Drumming ghost notes through the pattern of time.

The thought of the GHS killed her, because she was *so* close. She was an inch away from nothing, and yet the GHS persisted.

In a better world, there would be stories of knights going out into the wilderness to slay the Grand Hidden Something. These silvery bastards would gut everything until all that was left was absolute silence, an absolute rejection of somethings.

No body, no thoughts, no fear, no—

No no no no no.

Vee wept.

Want.

Desire.

Need.

It was still swirling inside of her. And maybe, just maybe, she could kill it. She thought that she could. She could be the knight. She could be the one who destroys the GHS and goes back to the village to sing of the triumphs of battle.

Only, *want* was slippery. It was conniving.

Or no. No, it was like your nose—cleverly edited out of sight by your own brain.

Vee considered the fundamental nature of this beast, the one that had wrapped itself around her very bones, her DNA, and focused her mind in the blackness to rid herself of it.

Her eyes went pink.

Then: white light.

She gasped, thrashing.

Voices she couldn't understand spoke.

No no no, I was so close.

"I was so fucking close!"

TWENTY-SEVEN

It was Wren who made the suggestion, at first.

Mom was out of the laundry closet and was acting strangely. She wept when Cossel opened the door, frozen in place. Soon though, she blinked. Then, she turned her head, saw her family, and screamed.

"I was so fucking close!"

They laughed. They didn't know what else to do.

It was all very tiring for the rest of them. Wren was thankful her father took charge of her.

For whatever reason, Wren never did like her mother—so, to watch her father gruffly pick her up, muttering to himself, was no great loss. She liked the idea that his grip hurt her.

From her lips, out of nowhere, she said, "Maybe you should slap her one, Dad. Right across the face."

Her father smiled, glowering down at his wife. Her head lolled back and forth, her pupils pinpricks, as if they refused to register the light. He winded his arm back, a side-eye toward Wren for her approval. His arm snapped like a rubber band, leaving a red palm print across her face.

She cried more.

"Enough of this," he said. "Maybe she just needs a good fucking."

Wren laughed at that. "Show her what you're made of, champ."

Ed dragged her down the hall, her eyes rolled back into her head. Wren turned to Cossel and smiled wickedly. "Mom's about to get got."

"Yeah, she is."

"How's your leg?"

Vee screamed, a throat-shredding holler separated from a thin wall. Her children shook their heads.

"Not great," said Cossel. "Better." He shifted his weight when he said it, keeping his eyes down low.

"I still have to do an impression," said Wren.

"Yeah? What were you thinking?"

She nodded to their parents' door. "Who else?"

"Okay," said Cossel. He giggled. The idea amused him. *Of all people…?* "Show me what you got."

Wren thought for a moment. "No, I have an idea."

She took him by the hand and led him to her room. She sat him on the bed. "Can you hear them?"

Cossel listened. His mother's screams had become moans, and his father's horrible grunts became a series of dry barking coughs. He tapped the rhythm of his father's thrusts on his leg. "Yeah, I hear it."

"Okay," said Wren. "We can do it like them. We can do an impression."

"Us, together?"

"Sure," said Wren. "Why not? You like to fuck, I like to fuck. But it's not really even us doing it. You have to call me Vee and I have to call you Ed. We have to make their noises too."

"You're my sister," said Cossel. But even as he said it, his protest was weak. The sentence came out as a bored declaration.

Wren nodded. "We've got nothing else to do."

Cossel agreed. "I suppose we don't."

Before he could finish his sentence, Wren had stripped nude. She was very pretty, he had to admit. *She looks like Mom*, he thought.

His own clothing came off in a pile. Cossel was comparatively sexually inexperienced, having had sex twice with a girlfriend he had lost in two months. Still, with the burden of virginity lifted, he felt a freedom in his lovemaking.

Wren laid on the bed and she tapped her slender fingers on the wall. She kept her parent's time like a metronome. With the other hand, she licked her fingers and masturbated.

"I'm wet, Cos. Are you hard?"

"Yeah, I'm hard."

"Okay, get up here. Can you do Dad's moan-grunt thing?"

"I think so," he said, as he slid his penis into his sister. He held still, listening for his father's rhythm like a new kid waiting to jump into a game of double dutch. *One, two, three, four…*

He commenced thrusting, hard and deep. His penis tingled inside of his sister, threatening to explode. When she moaned—a cartoonish impression of their mother—he remembered that this was not simply play. This was work too.

"HARGH! HARGH HARGH!" he bellowed. His impression was so good that even Wren, now flushed with her eyes closed, forgot to moan. Soon though, she got back into character.

"I wanna cum, Wren."

"Call me Vee."

"I wanna cum, Vee."

"You need to wait, Ed. Please, wait for Dad. Try to time it with Dad."

He pumped into her, measuring his strokes so that they were the mirror of his father. He did not know if he could hold on much longer. In fact, he was sure that he couldn't.

Luckily, his father's pace quickened. *He's getting close*, he thought.

He grabbed Wren by the waist and pounded her harder. He opened his lungs and let loose the howl-bark that he'd come to know so well through the walls of his room.

"Should I pull out?" he gasped, his muscles already tensing.

"What's the point?"

Cossel came. His body relaxed as he emptied himself of his ejaculate into his sister.

He rolled over and wiped his brow. "Did you cum?"

"No," said Wren. She reached out a hand to touch his. "But that's okay, Mom never does either." With her other hand, she touched herself. "Can you stay with me until I cum?"

"Sure, sis," he said.

The house was quiet, except for the gentle schlicking of mother and daughter—too faint for either party to hear. When Wren finished, Cossel got dressed and left for his room.

A sense of wrongness tugged at his mind. But it was easy to tuck away, so he did just that.

TWENTY-EIGHT

Ed woke early, he was not accustomed to waking early, but he did so anyway. It was to be the last week and he was not sure if there was going to be a fair end to any of this. So, he woke early and paced back and forth. Vee slept, still as death. Every few minutes, she jerked in her sleep as if having a nightmare. He smiled and thought of jumping on her chest and screaming, but didn't.

It was Sunday morning and Mr. Cormorant would be back.

Groceries showed up at their doorstep—the amounts larger and larger each week. This day, near the end of their tenure in the house, was the largest amount yet. He opened the door and brought each bag in. Part of him considered letting Vee put them away when the bags were on the table but he just looked at the Product, sighed, and did it anyway. *Vee was having a rough time*, he thought abstractly. *She might appreciate this.*

It was six AM and he wasn't sure when Mr. Cormorant was coming, but he assumed it would be at exactly the right time.

Internally, the strangely dressed man had become a sort of folk hero millionaire. Something between Elon Musk and the Monopoly man. Ed thought that the next time he saw Mr. Cormorant, he'd shake his hand, look him in the eye, and ask to work for him. Whatever he did for business, it was the right kind of business. They'd eaten like kings for the last month. Ed didn't know a lot but he knew for the last three weeks his family was living better than most.

Ed poured a glass of orange juice and sipped. He listened for rustling upstairs, but otherwise said and did nothing. It wasn't important. Before the Product, he would've been anxious, he would've been scared. But now? He knew the time would come. Minutes, hours, whatever—they all would pass. And he'd be in the kitchen, drink in hand, calmly waiting, lost inside his own head.

It wasn't for another two and a half hours that the door opened. Mr. Cormorant sashayed into the house and went straight to the machine.

Ed was dumbstruck at how fast it happened. He forgot his plan in an instant.

The Psychographist turned to him. "Good morning, Ed. How are you?"

"Good," he said. "I mean, well. No, good."

"One more week. Will you be glad to leave?"

"No," he said, honestly. "I'd stay here for another year like this, if I could."

"For how much?"

Ed stammered. "I—I—I don't know. A hundred thousand, maybe?"

"So, you'd stay in this house with the Product for a month for fifty thousand, but a year for a hundred thousand." The Psychographist approached him, looming. "Your negotiation tactics need work, Ed. You're selling yourself short."

"I know, I know," he said. He hit himself on the head. "Stupid of me. I should've asked for more." He paused. "But how much more?"

Mr. Cormorant shrugged. "Why not everything?"

"Everything?" Ed smiled. "Would you give me everything?"

"No," he said, shaking his head slowly. "But it's a start. Don't sell yourself short or else you'll fill your life with woe. And when you want to go, you will stand still, stuck at port, unable to move forward. Think of the you you wanna be."

He nodded his head, the Psychographist's words worming their way into his brain.

"Thank you," he said. "Thank you."

Mr. Cormorant's powdered cheeks were cut with a smile.

Ed remembered. "I wanted to ask… I wanted to ask if you're hiring. At Cormorant/Carmichael. I think you could use a guy like me."

"Why is that?"

"I'm a hard worker. I do what I'm told. I believe in your business."

"Is that so?"

"Yes," he said. "It's true. After this is done, I think you should hire me. I can help."

The Psychographist rolled his eyes back into his head. "We shall see." Then, he turned to see the family roused from their bed and coming down the stairs.

"Mr. Cormorant," said Vee. "Good morning."

"I hope I didn't wake you," he said.

"No, no, no," said Vee. "I was just getting up."

Wren nudged her brother. "We'd been up for a little too."

The siblings laughed. Ed did not know what about, but he thought little of it except a quiet delight at their good humor.

"The gang's all here. How has the last week been?"

"Good," said Ed. "Great."

"Not as good," said Vee. "I can't explain it. But not as good."

"I'm sorry to hear that. When did it stop feeling as good?"

Vee's voice was dreamy, a thousand miles away. "Maybe when I cut my fingers off? Maybe a little after. When I stayed in the closet for a day. It was good in some ways. Almost peaceful and I just kinda… drifted off. I didn't even need my piss bucket. But, something went wrong. I saw—I saw—" Tears welled in her eyes.

"It's okay," said Mr. Cormorant. "I know exactly what you saw. There, there." He turned his head to Wren and Cossel. "As for you two, how are you? Have you been making the best of your time together?"

Cossel blushed and his sister mussed his hair. "You could say that. We started fucking."

"No shit?" said Vee.

"Is that safe?"

Vee shrugged. "Nothing else to do in here."

"That's fair," said Ed. He looked at his daughter for a moment, then shook his head. "Maybe we could too?"

"I don't wanna fuck you, Dad. You're too old for me."

"Fine, fine."

Mr. Cormorant nodded through all of this and then said, "I'm sad to say this experiment will be ending soon. I hope it has been a fruitful experience. I've been watching you. I've been observing you. And I'm proud to say that we at the office are *very* excited about the results."

"What are the results?" asked Cossel.

"Many, many million points of data, my boy. A banal revelation of the human mind and spirit. Nothing to worry yourself over. For now, in your last week, I want you to consider your next task. Are you ready, Hoyers?"

Ed nodded. He yelled, "Ready, sir!"

The Psychographist waved his white-gloved hands around in the air like a stage magician attempting sleight of hand. "Alright then, this last week is an easy week, in some ways, but much more difficult in others."

Ed watched his hands. It was all he saw.

"There is only one task this week," he said. "And I believe you are up for it. You have proven yourself as extremely adept subjects so far, and I want you to know that I am happy. You have made me happy. Together, you have worked to uncover the language of humanity. The magnet that lies at the center of your chests. Your hearts. And now, all you have to do is look around the room and choose one person in your family to kill.

And then, when you have picked them. You have to kill them."

Cossel said, "That's it?"

"That's it."

"Sounds easy enough," said Ed.

Vee yawned, stretched. For a brief moment, she saw the bandages wrapped around her hands and her vacant mask slipped. But after shutting her eyes and biting her lips, she said, "Yes, that sounds fine."

"Whatever," said Wren. "Go out with a bang, right?"

The Product hummed.

They turned their heads in unison, like synchronized puppets.

The LED turned red.

TWENTY-NINE

That night they sat around the table, drinking.

Cossel hadn't drank since the night he had his accident and in some ways the rush of alcohol was unwelcome. But it became easy not to think when it hit his lips. There was a task at hand, and it was imperative they worked together.

"Are we religious, Dad?"

"How do you mean?"

"I mean, do we believe in heaven? If one of us is killed, can we believe they went to heaven?"

"I don't know, Cos. That's a big question. I'm not religious, your mother isn't either. But we're not anti-religion. We just never connected to it. We didn't grow up with it like some people. It's better to think that we're going to heaven though. We can say that we're religious if you want."

Cossel nodded. "I think it'd be easier to kill someone if I knew they were going to heaven."

"Does it matter?" said his sister. "Either way they're dead. Zip, done."

"It would make it easier after," said Vee. "I'd be sad having to kill someone."

The family drank in shared solemnity.

Ed said to Wren, "I think for the purposes of this conversation, let's say that we are religious. For the sake of this task."

"Fine," said Wren. "I'm religious!"

"But now we have to decide who it'll be," said Vee. "I don't want it to be me."

"No one wants it to be them, Mom," said Cossel, his cheeks rosy. "None of us want to die. That's why we're religious now. We believe in heaven and shit."

"You can't fuck your sister in heaven," said Wren.

"In *my* heaven, you can do anything you want."

"Sounds like heaven," said Wren.

"So, okay, we've established that there's now a heaven. We still have to make the choice," said Ed. "How should we do this?"

Vee lit a cigarette and took a long drag. "What if we went around and said why we shouldn't be the one to die?"

"That could work," said Ed.

"I don't like that," said Cossel. "Everybody has a reason to live. I think we should go around the table and talk about who we think most deserves to die."

"I don't think anyone deserves to die," said Wren. "Maybe we could just discuss the pros and cons of each as a group."

"Okay," said Ed. "I like that. Let's start with me. I think on one side, I have a lot to live for. If someone dies in this family, the family will still persist and there will need to be an adult leader. Someone who has had the authority before and knows what to do with it. Also, I have the best chance at earnings here as I have the most work history. Mr. Cormorant and I talked about me coming aboard full time after this."

"Honey, that's great news." She shook her head. "Who would've thought so many good things would come from you getting fired?"

Ed laughed. "Oh, I wasn't fired."

"You weren't?"

"No, no," said Ed. "That was a lie. I quit. I got fed up and walked out. I was tired of being a doormat. That's why we're here. Because I grew a spine."

Vee's lips trembled. "You quit your job?"

"Yes. And I couldn't be happier."

She nodded. "I feel like I should be angrier."

"Not very responsible, Dad," said Wren.

"But it's led to a new job. It's led to potentially better income."

"We could get a better place. With all the money coming in. That's something," said Cossel.

"But Dad's old," said Wren. "He's the oldest of everyone here. Even a year or so older than Mom, right?"

"Right."

"He's experienced the most out of life and I think it'd make sense for him to be killed. There's no better option is there?"

Ed ground his teeth but didn't say anything. "Alright then, how about you Wren?"

"I was just about to leave this town. I think I'm poised as the person here who has the most to gain from living. Check this: I am going to be going to college. I will have a new fifty thousand dollars to pay for it. I plan on going and getting a real degree, not a fake liberal arts thing. If I make it out of here, in one week, I'm truly most likely to succeed."

"Sure, but you've never shown great aptitude at anything before," said Vee. "I could see you falling down on the job pretty fast. School isn't just expensive, it's a lot of work. I just don't see you putting in the work."

"That's right, hon," said Dad. "You've been lazy for most of your teen years. Why do you think a summer job changes any of that? I think if we killed you, we could get you to heaven before disappointment sets in."

Wren shook her head. 'That's bullshit and you know it. I work *hard*."

"Yeah, you work hard," said Cossel. "But for how long?"

"Fine," she said. "You've had your say but if I do make it though, my chance at earnings are a lot higher than any of you. I could support this family alone!"

Ed shook his head. "No, you couldn't. You wouldn't even be here. The fact that you're planning to leave isn't going to help anyone. If you leave, someone in this family will be dead and you won't be around to help. That's no bueno, Wren. I think it'd be easier on me if you were to die, personally." He added the last word as reassurance.

"Moving on," he continued. "Vee."

She extinguished her cigarette in her glass. "I don't think I've really lived yet. Think of me, as your mother. I had you kids young. I didn't get to see the world. I didn't get to do anything but be a mother. Don't get me wrong, I love you kids… but still. I'd love to be able to travel, to do drugs, to fuck strangers. I'd love to do any and all of that stuff. But instead, I'm here. I don't get to cry. I don't get to despair. I have to be Mom. I don't think I deserve to die because I haven't really lived. And as your mother, I think you should think about me."

"I think I want to kill you just for that manipulative bull-shit," said Wren.

"Wren's right, hon. That was a little over the top. I didn't get to live either."

Vee bared her teeth. "It is not the same for us. You take that back. You do not know what it was like."

"I remember being tired. I remember having to work my ass off," he raised his voice gradually. Soon, it was a roar. "I remember having to put up with your post-whatever bullshit. Listening to you whine and cry about everything you'd never be. But guess what, honey, I never got to be anything either!"

"Kids, we should kill your father," said Vee. "He's being an asshole."

"I think Mom's still old enough to be worth killing," said Cossel. "Sorry, Mom."

"Mom's always acting like a victim," said Wren. "This is her thing. She barely works because of 'depression.' Everyone's depressed Mom, not just you. They still find ways to work."

"That's—that's not true. I just have trouble getting hours, that's all."

"That's bullshit and you know it, Vee. If you wanted to, you could do more. Your brain is all fucked. It's been fucked since you had the kids. We could put you down like a sick dog and everyone would be happier."

All three of them stared at Vee, eyes rimmed with hate. Tears crawled down her cheeks. She couldn't meet any of their eyes. "Fine," she choked. "If you want me to die… maybe I'll just…"

"God, Mom. Just stop. It's Cossel's turn now."

Cossel cleared his throat. "I'm the youngest," he said. "I think that's reason enough for me to live a long and happy life. I don't want to die here. I have dreams and wants. I made a list of them. I think Dad should die. That's what makes sense to me. With the money we have from Mr. Cormorant we should be more than fine, right? Wren will be leaving for school and then it'll just be Mom and me if Dad's dead. That's a lot cheaper. Less mouths to feed. We could even get a smaller place, if we needed to."

"On the other hand," said Ed. "Because you've lived the shortest, you might also be the least attached to living."

"That's true," said Vee. "You'll always be my baby boy, but if I'm being honest, my time with you was the hardest. I actually did try to kill myself after you were born. Sometimes I think that's all I'm trying to do now—kill myself over and over again."

"God, Mom, shut up," said Wren, disgusted. "Cossel also has a bum leg. He'll need to get that fixed so a lot of money will have to go to that if we keep him around. That's a waste, in my opinion."

Cossel looked at his sister with hurt eyes.

"Also, we started fucking, which is going to make his life in high school miserable if anyone finds out. Because I'm the older sibling, it'll likely cause confused feelings and ripples of abuse later in his life too. Sorry, Cos, I fucked you up good. You might as well say good night while you still can."

"Those are good points," said Ed. "Those are great points. Cos, how are your legs feeling?"

"It's just the left one," he said. "It feels fine. I don't even have to have surgery, you know?"

"But would you be willing to go without it?"

"Definitely. I was never going to be an athlete. I don't need my leg. It's just a leg. I can walk mostly fine without it. See?" He got out of his kitchen chair and walked around the living room in a circle, doing his best to disguise his limp. "Barely noticeable. I can get around just fine."

The rest of the family squinted, examining his every movement.

Ed sighed. "Maybe," he said. "Maybe. I'd just hate to see all that money go to waste. If we can save money by killing you, that'd be better for the whole family. Do you understand, son?"

"I do," he said. "But I think we should think on it longer."

"Why?"

"Because there are better people to kill than me and I'd hate for you to make your mind up too early and lose a son. You remember that, right? I'm your son. We're the only men here. I think that's important to you, right?"

"Oh God, you're as bad as Mom," said Wren. "Wah, wah, wah—always the victim."

"I was pregnant when I was your age," said Vee, her words a whip. "Don't for a second think you know anything about anything."

"It's embarrassing how readily you threw your life away."

"That's why we both deserve a second chance. One less kid could help us reconnect."

"But what about one less spouse?"

"What?"

Wren smiled wickedly. "You're a man, Dad. I know how men think. Look at Mom, do you still think about her when you jack off?" She reached out to his leg, rubbing it. "I'm younger. But I'm not the only one. There's a lot of younger women out there. Or men. Have you fucked a man before, Daddy?"

"No," he said. "Not yet."

"You could get rid of Mom and give it a try. Orgies, Dad. You could have orgies."

"I've fucked him twice a day for the last three weeks!" screamed Vee. "There's nothing wrong with our sex life. God, you paint people into fucking boxes, don't you? First, I'm depressed so that's all I am. Second, he wants to fuck other people, so that's all he wants. We're more than that, Wren. We're all more than that."

"Your mother's right," said Ed. "We're all more than a couple bullet points. There are plenty of reasons to kill or not kill each other. Let's sleep on it. We have a week to decide."

Cossel said, "I have a proposal too."

His mother sounded tired, worn down. "Go ahead," she moaned through tears.

"I think we should wait for the last day. Saturday. Whoever has to die should get to live out a full week."

"I like that," said Ed. "We have time. We should enjoy it."

They all agreed to that.

THIRTY

Cossel and Wren fucked in a daze of musky sublimation. When they finished, they also smoked and drank from their parents' stash of ever-refilling liquor—courtesy of Mr. Cormorant.

"So, you think it's going to be you?" asked Wren.

"Probably," said Cossel. "I don't think it should be though."

"Me neither."

"But you said—"

"That was part of the game. We had to say something. I don't think we should die. We're the youngest."

Cossel was confused, but he had been confused a lot lately. His mind didn't work the same. He was short on insight. For some reason, the world around him was laced in a thick fog. He was not sure what was happening at any given time. On the bed, beside his sister, he wondered if this was how babies felt. Like little machines meant for nothing but sensory intake.

He said, "What do you think then?"

"I think between the two of us, we can kill one of them early. When they don't expect us."

"I didn't even think of that," he said. The idea came to him clearly and his heart beat with excitement. "I've wanted to kill Dad for a while now."

"Yeah? Why?"

"I don't know," he admitted.

"I'd rather kill Mom, but I'm not picky. Mom would be easier, I think. We could kill Dad too though."

"I never thought of that either. Would we get their share of the money though? Or would I just be put into foster care and have my money taken away? I really wanted that car."

"Good point," said Wren. "I think we should just kill one then or else we're setting ourselves up to be fucked over."

"Okay, well I'd rather be left with Mom than Dad."

"Mom doesn't have a job though."

"But she lets me get away with more. It'll be easy, I think."

"Her head is scrambled. Have you heard her talk?"

Cossel thought for a moment. "Have you listened to any of us? We're all fucked up." The words were perfunctory, but the fog lifted as he said them. "Holy shit. What is happening to us?"

Wren, for a moment, caught a whiff of the same revelation. She moved her naked body further away from her brother.

Both of them thought for a moment.

Whatever was on the tips of their tongues vanished.

"We should kill Dad," said Cossel. "It's the best way."

"Fine, I don't care that much. As long as it's not me."

"Or me."

"That too."

"When do we do it?" asked Cossel.

Wren smiled. "I have a plan."

Ed watched porn on the family television, lazily masturbating. Sometimes, he would hear the Product, but he'd been hearing the Product since before he could walk. Everyone had.

Do it, do it, do it.

"I will, I will," he muttered.

On the screen, a trio of men were having sex with a slender blonde whose mascara was running in black strings down her face. "I've never fucked someone so hard that they looked like that," he said.

An image of Wren, upstairs, flashed in his mind.

He considered that. "So she is. But she's probably fucking Cossel right now."

Join in. Show the kids what you can do.

His cock was hard, he played with it, stroking it on the couch until a bubble of precum appeared at the tip.

"I really shouldn't," he said, gasping. "I shouldn't be doing any of this." His cock wilted. He turned to the Product, painted in its red glow. "I think you're pushing us too far. We can't do this," he said. "None of this is right."

The machine hummed louder.

Ed shook his head, then scratched at the sides of it. "What is going on here? Get out of my head!"

But he couldn't get it out. Its stinger was already buried deep. He saw himself, again, his hands wrapped around his children's throats, his dead wife festering on the floor. Somewhere, someone was laughing at him.

If Ed were being honest, he always felt like that. Since the beginning of his life. He lived with the sense that someone smarter than him was watching and laughing at his every decision. That he was a comedy of errors for some better version of himself. Like the hum though, this feeling became so persistent it was innocuous.

"I think I need to leave the house," he said. "I think we all need to leave."

These were new thoughts though. In some moments he thrashed in terror at who he was, and other times, he was as docile and vacant—effectively lobotomized. Sometimes, he would wake at night and scream and then Vee would scream too and he would see the fear in her face too, but then they would fuck instead of talk. And then whatever it was that scared them was gone.

New house, new car, new job. You're going to be someone important, said the Product.

"Right," he said. He thought of those things, pictured them, and agreed. "You're totally right." His eyes glazed over. He grabbed his cock.

A new video began to play.

Vee laid in the darkness of the laundry room, again. She drank in the blackness and worshiped it. She tried to give it all her love and hoped that it would give some back. An explanation, a reasoning. She was so close before.

After their conversation in the morning, she wanted to vanish into the darkness again and shed everything that plagued her.

Murder my children? Murder my husband?

There was something inside of her, so deep that it was now her core. She hoped to find this and reveal it, show it to the world and herself and her family (most of all her family) so that they'd know she was not broken—that there was a truth mortared in her cracks.

She sat and thought, clearing her mind. The phantom joints of her missing fingers traveled up her arm and her shoulder. Now those were phantoms too. Then, the same happened to her feet and torso, her head. It was when her heartbeat dissipated that she almost gasped, fell out of it, but she remained steadfast in her determination.

Everything was gone.

There was only blackness. An endless, cold void that was both comforting and terrifying. Its vastness consumed her, and she consumed it.

The two of them consumed each other. Her gobbling its vastness. It chewing up her hunger. Here was an endless cycle—of two starved mouths feasting.

Vee opened her eyes.

Her breath hitched.

The closet blackness was not the same as the void blackness. It was an imitation, a falsehood.

A voice crept into her brain. *You've seen behind the curtain. What do you do now?*

"That's all it is," she said. Her voice dead and tired, her eyes dry. "There's nothing more."

Nope.

"Okay," she said.

THIRTY-ONE

Late in the night, Cossel awoke.

Wren was standing over his bed, shaking his dead foot. "Get up," she whispered.

"Fuck, don't do that. That hurts."

She shrugged, as if the notion of pain was a meaningless abstract to her.

"We've got to do it now. It's time."

"Time for what?"

Wren glared at him.

"Oh, that. Yeah. What do I do?"

"Take this." She laid a knife on the bed. "We both have to do it, we have to do it together. He's stronger than us, I think, so we'll have to do our best to end him immediately. There's no other way."

"Okay," said Cossel.

Cossel got out of bed. The floor was cold, and his feet twitched. It was dark so he had to be extra careful, extra considerate of his leg.

The two children held knives in their hands, dressed in their sleepwear. Wren said no more.

They crept out of the bedroom and into the hallway. Cossel could hear both of them breathing. In and out, in and out. A gentle, yet hoarse wind.

Moonlight slid in through the windows and kissed each of them with its blessings.

This is a beautiful night, thought Cossel, idly. *This is a good night to do this.*

Wren was in front, she pushed on their parent's bedroom door with the tips of her fingers—very gently.

Cossel held his breath.

The house reverberated with the squeal of hinges. "We should go back," he whispered.

Wren only waved her hand to urge him forward.

The door opened from a slit. Cossel peered in from behind Wren, his eyes adjusting to the relative darkness.

He could see his parent's bed. The floor was messy, covered in piles of unwashed clothes and empty beer cans. They'd also taken to stuffing their cigarette butts into these cans, creating an overwhelmingly acrid smell of stale beer and tobacco.

Cossel stepped carefully over the floor. He adjusted the grip on his knife. Wren had hers at the ready, point out.

When they both stood over the bed, they could barely make out the shapes in the blankets. Dad's head was all that was visible, everything else was a twisted mess.

Wren didn't wait though. The knife slashed through the air.

Cossel was right behind her. But as their father thrashed and screamed, and Wren's knife cut through his skin, the blankets came off.

He smiled with glee as he tore into his father's leg, taking careful aim at the kneecap.

But a thought persisted, separate from his actions.

The space beside his father—empty.

Where's Mom? he wondered.

THIRTY-TWO

The Product looked nearly inconspicuous in the living room. It was nothing more or less than any other piece of furniture. Black and strangely jagged; like a monolith chipped and eroded by time. Burnt to ashes and more.

Vee stared at it with intense eyes.

"I have lost three fingers," she said.

The Product didn't speak to her.

"I will never have them back. I ate them and shit them out. Did you know that I went through my own shit? I pulled it out and looked for parts that were recognizable to me as fingers, but I couldn't find any. I think you're the reason this happened. I don't think I would've eaten my fingers if it weren't for you."

The machine remained silent.

"Something isn't right," she continued. "And I can't tell what it is. But I know that people don't usually eat their fingers. Families do not usually plot to kill each other. Although, that is what we are doing. I think something is wrong and I think you're the cause." Vee took a deep breath. "I was going to kill myself, you know. I was going to kill myself because I thought I was the problem. I've always thought I was the problem, since I was a kid but when I was in that blackness, I saw the center of everything. I don't think I'm the problem. Or rather, the problem is not limited merely to me."

The machine's LED light ebbed and flowed, pulsing crimson.

"I think I must thank you for making me eat myself," she said. "Because if I had not, I would not have understood absence. I think I've been fighting against absence my whole life, trying to fill an empty well. And now, having seen the opposite, I realize that from birth I was never given the choice. I have been a machine—just like you—a machine that swallows stimuli. And I don't want to be that anymore."

Vee's hand came from behind her back. Her fingers went white holding the hammer.

"There was a song about this, I think. 'If I had a Hammer.' It's an old song, at least to people of my generation. For you though, I suspect you are very old, Carmichael. It might still be new to you."

The machine said nothing, and Vee raised the hammer and stepped forward.

"I'm going to teach us both about absence. But first you."

She reared back and slammed the hammer down.

The Product screeched, a supernatural scream of static. It pierced her ears. They were ringing, but she swung again. And again. And again.

Chunks of black plastic fell to the ground, cracking like an eggshell. Dark goo bubbled from its wounds and dripped onto the floor and began to evaporate immediately.

It made loud honking noises, distorted. And Vee kept swinging and swinging and swinging and swinging. Soon, the small black tower was nothing but rubble, soaked in charcoal spit. It smelled like space, like ozone and burnt toast and irony blood.

Vee gasped, as if dunked in ice water. She looked around her, at her hands, and tried to scream. She looked at the machine and couldn't breathe.

Footsteps.

She looked up to the stairs to see Wren and Cossel, covered in blood, running toward her.

The hammer was still in her hand.

The fog was lifted.

The Product was gone.

She looked to her kids and said, "I'm sorry. I can't do this."

And before she could hear their response, or see the puzzled looks on their faces, she turned the hammer's claw toward her head, took a deep breath, and sent it through the front of her skull.

Vee fell forward, the hammer's teeth stuck in her brain.

Two lights died.

THIRTY-THREE

Cossel and Wren could not hold each other at first, because they knew what they had done.

Cossel sat on the couch, separating himself from his sister. Wren remained on the stairs, weeping into her hands. Their flesh repelled each other.

For an hour, in the night, they sat as quietly as they could. The fog lifted and there were many things to think about.

"We killed Dad," said Cossel finally.

"Why did we do that?"

"I don't know. We wanted to."

"Was it the money?"

"I don't know. We're going to jail now, right?"

"I think so. You might get lucky though. You're still a minor. It's not gonna look good for me when I tell them I—I don't even want to talk about it."

"Me neither. We don't have to mention that to anyone."

"I'm so sorry, Cos," she said. "That's abuse. I *abused* you."

He replayed their coupling in his head and felt a deep sense of revulsion. "It's like... I don't know what it's like. We weren't right in the head."

She motioned to the dead machine. "That thing fucked us up."

"Mom's dead too," said Cossel. "What are we going to do?"

"I don't know. I don't fucking know."

"We don't have parents anymore," he said, choking. "We're fucking alone. What do we even do? Who do we even call?"

"The police?"

"We can't call the police. We're gonna be taken away immediately."

"We can't run from this either. There's no fucking way. We're stuck."

They fell back into solemn silence. Soon, the gray light from early morning poured in through their windows.

"Mr. Cormorant will be back," said Wren. "He's going to come back for us."

Cossel shivered. "I thought he was a bad dream."

"He's not. I saw him a couple of times. In the house."

"Me too. I didn't want to say it but I did too."

"I don't think he's here now," said Wren. "I think he was tied to that *thing* over there. Somehow. Like that it allowed him to influence us more or something."

"I can't believe any of this. None of this is real, right?" But as soon as he said it, his eyes looked over to his mother. Her eyes were closed, permanently frozen in a wince. Blood had pooled and congealed around her head.

"We should call someone," she said. "We can't live here with the—" She stumbled over the word. "Bodies."

"This is the worst day of my life," he said. "This is the worst month of my life."

"I'm sorry, Cos. Me too."

"I wanna go for a walk," he said, suddenly. "I haven't been outside."

"Change your clothes," she said.

He went upstairs and quickly pulled on a t-shirt, jeans, and a hoodie, washing the blood off his hands in the sink.

"You want to come with?"

"No," said Wren. "Maybe later. I need to think."

"Okay, sis," he said. Then, added, "Don't do anything stupid, okay?"

"I won't."

Outside, the air was crisp and cool, and the sun had risen, bathing Springfield in golden light. The houses that lined Cossel's street reminded him of something from a painting. Norman Rockwell, some saccharine dose of Americana. He thought about that while he walked, what it'd be like to live life in a painting.

The air felt good in his lungs. It was better than he could have ever imagined. The air inside his home had become stale and fetid—but he hadn't noticed it until now.

He wasn't sure what he was supposed to do. So, he walked.

Springfield was the type of town that was easy to walk in.

Halfway through his walk, he leaned over into some hedges and vomited. Then, he kept walking.

For some reason, he decided to walk to Grady's house. It wasn't on the way to anything, but it was close enough that there was no reason not to. He didn't plan on knocking or saying hello, he just wanted to see something familiar—something that he once treasured.

Grady's house was small, like Cossel's, but better maintained. It was free standing, one story, and while there was little room, it did have a modest front yard with a well-groomed garden. Grady's mom loved to garden. Whenever Cossel came to Grady's house she'd be under a stack of gardening books. She always used to call the plants by their Latin names too, as if those words carried a magic and specificity that English simply couldn't. Cossel's heart ached for those memories.

How am I ever going to talk to anyone again? he wondered. Normal people care about normal things. They have normal experiences. *I'm not normal now. Not anymore.*

Cossel's muscle memory took him to the house. It felt good to have these memories.

But the house did not look the same. The house was different. *The yard was different.*

He squinted, trying to place what was wrong.

There was the garden, first. Weeds had overtaken it. Long thin lines of vegetation reached out from the earth and strangled flowers. They spilled out onto the sidewalk in front of the house, as if trying to escape their own doom.

Unruly, unkempt.

That's not right. That's not how I remember it, he thought.

Then, there was the house itself. Two windows, one always obscured by curtains. The one with curtains was Grady's mom's room. The other looked into their living room.

Something was wrong there.

He took a step forward, looking back and forth. A nagging fear pulled at his brain. *I'll be discovered,* he thought.

And the fact that he carried this burden alone with Wren made his heart sink. Slinking up the steps to Grady's home, he never felt heavier.

When he got to the front window, he peered in carefully. He checked his phone. It was a weekday, and Grady would be getting ready for school. His house was usually alive at this time. He and his mother used to have breakfast together. She worked early at the hospital and always made it a point to sit together. He remembered because he used to make fun of him for it.

But the living room was empty. The TV was on but no one was watching. And what was that dark shape in the corner?

Cossel took a step back. The sun's glare obscured it, but when he ducked his head just right, he saw what looked like an obsidian obelisk, a blue LED running down its front like a rivulet of alien blood.

Oh no.

The house was still and silent.

If he listened close, he could hear the same ethereal hum.

No no no no.

He backed away from the window.

But just in time, to see one last thing.

A flash of movement.

A woman.

Grady's mother.

He thought, youthfully, that he should wave to her, explain why he was looking into her windows. But she wasn't looking at him. Her head was tilted down, her eyes a blank slate. It was like she was looking at nothing, and nothing was looking right back at her.

But when he saw it, he started a lop-sided dash away from the house. He couldn't run, and he cursed his leg for that. But he went down the sidewalk, carefully hauling his limp foot, keeping his muscles tense to protect his knee, and tried to get as far away from Grady's house as he could.

He saw her face, unobscured by flare or shadows. For only a second.

She was covered in blood. Strings of tendon were hanging from her face.

Cossel could only guess where they came from.

THIRTY-FOUR

"Check this out," she said.

Cossel was pacing the floor, avoiding the spot where his mother lay dead. "What?"

"Online. People are talking about us?"

"Us?"

"Well, not us specifically. But they're talking about what's happening."

Cossel shook his head. "I don't think I want to hear this." His stomach churned. "Grady is dead."

Wren looked up at him with big, kind eyes. She said, "Hey, Cos. I'm sorry."

The words were warm, real. Cossel nodded. "Thanks, sis."

"Are you okay?"

"No. I keep thinking about... *things.*"

"Me too," she said. She held her arms across her chest, crossing them. "Are you okay being here with me?"

"Yeah, I guess," he said. He suppressed a shudder. He didn't like when she talked about it.

"Okay," she said. "It grosses me out too. I wish someone could burn those memories out of my head. You ever see that movie *Eternal Sunshine of the Spotless Mind*? That's what I want. If I could forget, I would. I'm sure you would too."

"We'll have to go to therapy," he said. "Not just for that though."

Both of them made a point not to look at their mother's corpse.

"No," agreed Wren. "Not just for that."

"What did you find there?"

"More comments, more posts. The whole town's gone crazy. We're eating each other alive. Sometimes, literally."

"What?" He thought back to Grady's house.

"We weren't the only focus group. Others, others like us, also are dealing with… shit. Mom might have saved us before it got worse."

"We're orphans. Our parents are dead," he said.

She blinked back tears of her own. "Yeah, I know. I *know*, Cos. But she destroyed the Product, and we snapped out of it. Other people, not everyone, but some people have destroyed the Product in their homes and they went back to normal."

"It wasn't us doing that stuff?"

"I hope not," said Wren. "I don't know. Maybe it was some part of us."

"I don't want to think about that. I don't want to think about some part of me wanting to do any of the things we did." He shook his head. "I remember I made a list. I made a list and I wanted to kill Dad. That's in writing."

"You should burn it."

"I might," said Cossel. He tried to place himself back into that moment and remember what he was feeling, who he thought he was. *Am I that same person? Am I the person who wanted to kill? Did I want to sleep with Wren?*

He couldn't answer the questions.

"It's just people like us who did the focus group. The people who could afford not to didn't see the point. Some of them have left."

"Where to?"

"Away."

"What about the cops?"

Wren flicked her thumb across her phone screen. "They can't keep up with what's going on. There's looting going on now. Rapes, murders, cannibalism. Here, catch." She threw him the phone. "Read that post."

Cossel lifted it to his face, his eyebrows arched. In one long paragraph, there was a delicious spectrum of misery and stream of conscious pleading.

I don't think we're going to make it through this we smashed the product two weeks in because FUCK that thing but we keep seeing HIM. He's everywhere and we can't get away. We don't know what to do. He keeps showing up everywhere, with the same sick smile. I see him in my dreams now. I see him everywhere. He whispers to me and tells me my future, he knows things about me that I don't know about myself. It's not right. It's not okay. He's trying to do something here and I don't know what it is. hubby was out walking the other day after we'd cleaned up the house and he saw what Springfield had become. Windows were boarded up and people were milling about the streets and their eyes were all fucked up and shit—like swirling. Like a cartoon or something. And Mr. Cormorant was walking around with them like nothing happened. Meanwhile, they were running after Mary Tell, the lady from the antique shop. They took everything she had on her, EVERYTHING. And when she was naked and scared, they just laughed. And then it got worse. One person started kicking her. Then another did too. They all were beating the shit out of poor Mary and hubby couldn't take it anymore. So he ran up to them and threw one of them to the ground. But they just got up and started chasing him. Meanwhile, others took their place around Mary and kept hurting her. Hubby made it home, but just barely. He said they saw others around him on the way back. Other people like him who weren't touched or taken, or not fully at least. We hear them at night, outside. They're jabbering nonstop. They're talking. They're making lists, pacing back and forth. We're scared. We're so FUCKING SCARED!!!

Cossel scrolled down to the next post.

Springfield is fucked. Police have lost all control. We've sold the house to an investment firm. Fuck this town and all these bullshit riots.

To the next.

C/C has bought out everything. It's done. There's nowhere to go. I'm posting this from a VPN and I don't feel safe. They, he, have their hands in everything. There's no way out. If you want to resist, look for an exit.

"The National Guard should be here, right?"

"You'd think," said Wren. "But they're not." She went to the window and peered out at their street. "We should leave."

Cossel stared down at his shoes. "Okay," he said. "Let's do it."

PRICE

THIRTY-FIVE

They packed light and spoke at a minimum. Cossel reached under his mattress to collect his Used Car Fund. It wouldn't last them forever, but it'd help.

A cold dread still crept into him. He remembered too much—him and Wren, matching his father's rhythm and sounds. He remembered the silver blade piercing his father's skin like it was nothing at all. The blood got everywhere. It was overwhelming. There was a brief moment, where the knife had gone in and out and the blood gushed hard on him that he paused. Frantic realization passed over his face, and then, panic subsided and was replaced with a warm calm. He stabbed the knife in again and again.

He felt sick to his stomach.

Dad was on the other side of that door, gutted. His blood was soaked into the mattress that he used to climb into ten short hours ago. He remembered that but he was too tired to cry, so he let it play in his mind on repeat as a sad elegy to whatever life he and his parents had. *Did he understand what was happening? Did he hate us?*

Cossel had the horrible thought that in those minutes of extreme pain and panic, that his father experienced the same clarity their mother did. That as he died, questions and shame flooded his mind with chaos.

It was not a pleasant thought.

After he packed, he stood outside of his parent's bedroom. Eyes closed, he reached out for the door and shut it.

Wren had the keys and was waiting. "We're gonna take my car even though it's a piece of shit. If anyone runs the plates, they'll at least see it belongs to me and not Mom and Dad." She frowned. "Let's get going."

Cossel got in the front seat. They'd both showered but didn't look any better for it. "Where are we gonna go?"

"We're gonna get out of Springfield, and we're gonna keep going until…"

Cossel let her trail off. Until was fine. He didn't have a better suggestion.

Down the street, he stared out the window. Wren was driving carefully, maybe too careful. "Do you think they'll know?"

"That we're not one of them?"

"Yeah."

"Maybe," she said. "Should I drive faster?"

"More erratically," he offered. "But be careful."

She jerked the wheel back and forth a little. "Like that?"

"Yeah. That's better."

He realized he was still holding his breath. Cossel sighed, took in a new lungful of air.

"Should we go downtown? See what it looks like?"

"No," said Cossel. "Let's not. Let's just leave."

Wren nodded. "Your wish is my command."

People walked the street. They looked light and airy, unconcerned. They moved without intent, more of a lackadaisical gallop to and fro—as if they were constantly testing the parameters of their own bodies. Sometimes, they would look at the car and a sick grin would cross their mouths.

"That's them," said Cossel. "That's the people they're talking about online."

"What should I do?"

"Nothing," said Cossel. "Or, I guess, don't draw attention to yourself."

"What would they do if they were driving?"

Cossel thought about that. He tried to search who he was only a day ago, when the Product's hum had overcome him. "Probably run into someone. Maybe a house. Drive into a ditch. Something like that."

"I don't want to do that."

"That's the trap. We can't. If we do any of those things, we might not be able to leave."

She jerked the wheel back and forth, swerving in and out of her lane. "This will have to do."

A man looked up behind them. At first, his face was quizzical, then it was furious. After a moment, it became as placid as a still lake. In the mirrors, Cossel could see a myriad of reactions. All of them were a mix of emotions, a kaleidoscope. It was as if one wasn't enough, or rather—that one could never be enough. The reactions didn't take, they were a muscle reaction that wasn't anything more than a perfunctory reflex. Cossel saw himself in every one.

"What's she doing?" asked Wren.

"What are you talking about?" He followed her gaze into the rearview mirror. "Oh shit."

A woman, mid-thirties, wearing a parka and pajama bottoms ran after the car. Her tongue hung out of her mouth and her pupils swirled like a hypnotists' pinwheel. Wren gasped.

"I had a dream about that," she said.

The woman howled as she picked her feet up off the ground and ran faster. Her head bobbed up and down, flailing side to side as if her neck was hanging on by a string of sinew.

More of them now.

Many more of them.

Cossel blinked.

Wren's hands gripped the steering wheel.

Now there were twenty, all of them in the same state of mismatched half-dress. They made noises—nonsense sounds. Animal sounds. Honking roars, cat-like hisses, inchoate moans.

Wren stomped down on the accelerator.

She turned a corner and as she sped through a residential street, the people began to straggle. Whether they stopped or lost interest, Cossel wasn't sure. But when he looked behind him, there were less of them. And then after another turn, there was less again.

"Thank god," he said.

"Yeah." Wren was breathing deep. "Jesus. What was that?"

And then: icy, cold words, spoken as if the red lips that made them were only an inch from their ears. "*That is form, function, and finality.*"

Wren screamed, she turned the wheel.

Cossel twisted back to see the Psychographist—but only for a second. The seatbelt pulled on his throat and in the space of a blink, Mr. Cormorant and his tuxedo were gone.

The car reeled, the brakes screeched, and the car went sliding. In front of them was a house, but there was no stopping at the speed they were going. The car blasted up the curb, careening through the air for a foot or two before they heard the bells of broken glass.

Wren said, "I'm so sorry."

Cossel didn't say anything. Everything was in slow motion. The hood had just burst through this family home's window. Next, it began to plow through the wall. Then, before the impact, the windshield buckled and there was nothing but white frosted cracks in front of them.

Both of them were jerked back and forth. Airbags exploded. The car stopped.

"Wren?" said Cossel. "Wren? Are you okay?"

His sister sat slumped over, unmoving.

"Sis?"

THIRTY-SIX

Cossel stepped out of the car and into the living room. Little pale legs stuck out from under the car.

"Are you okay?" he called out.

No answer.

He went to the driver's side door. "Hey, Wren. C'mon. We gotta get you out of here." He touched her neck, feeling for her pulse. He realized he hadn't touched her since they made love. Her skin was milky and soft to the touch. "Wake up, sis." He leaned on that last word as if it would do the heavy lifting of keeping him out of his memories. She was alive.

"Wren, Wren."

Her head rolled back and forth. He unbuckled her and pulled her out by her armpits, dragged her onto the shards of broken glass that peppered the living room. He stepped gingerly, avoiding any sudden twists or turns.

She opened her eyes. "Holy shit," she whispered. "Where are we?"

"Someone's house," he murmured.

He pointed to the kid under her car. "I think we killed that one."

"Boy or girl?"

"I don't know. Girl, I think. I didn't check her pussy."

Wren laughed at that. "Her family was probably slitting each other's throats like ours, right."

Cossel laughed, then stopped.

"What's wrong?"

He stood up and walked to the other room, drinking in his surroundings. Something was familiar here. A vibe, a tone, a *hum*.

"Wren, we gotta get outta here."

"Yeah?"

"Walk out onto the lawn."

"I'm dizzy."

"I know. It doesn't matter."

The Product stood in the corner of their kitchen, right beside the door to a basement coated with chipped white paint and deep knife wounds. He stepped back, as the thing's magnetic pull urged him forward.

Sit down, SHED.

The voice screamed in his head, and he twisted around and left the kitchen to the living room, limping to his sister. He helped her up.

"It's here," he said. "The Product is here. We gotta go. It's already fucking us up."

Wren's eyes went wide, and she got up on unsteady feet. "Okay, yeah. Let's go."

"Can we drive it?" asked Cossel.

"No, it's fucked. We have to walk." Even as she said it though, she was walking in zig-zags, barely able to stand.

"This isn't good," he said. He watched his sister struggle with the fundamentals of motion, just barely out of the range of the Product's influence.

There was no one in the street. He wasn't sure if there was anyone alive in the neighborhood. He thought about the girl under the car and wondered, *hoped*, that she'd already been dead when they drove through her living room.

What a sick thing to wish for, he chided himself.

Out in the street, he tried to figure something out. He tried to solve the problem. Dad had always told him that it was in his nature to solve problems.

He scanned the horizon.

"What's that?" he asked.

"What?" slurred Wren.

"That." He pointed into the distance, in the middle of the city. He could only make out the beginning of it, the base of it. Cranes. Long lines of cables lowering scaffolding—onto the jagged base of what looked to be a black skyscraper.

"We're leaving," he said. On the lawn across from him were two mountain bikes, decked out in the plastic accouterments of a kid's department store. "Can you ride a bike?"

"I think so," she said. She rubbed her temples. "Yeah, I can."

"Okay, then. Let's go."

They pedaled down the road as fast as they could, feeling the constraints of the bikes' size. Still, movement was better than no movement. They kept pushing with seemingly endless amounts of adrenaline. Wren trailed behind her brother but managed to keep the handlebars straight.

"They're building a big one," he yelled. "A huge one."

Wren didn't say anything. Her head was killing her. She tried to think but couldn't consider more than one thought at a time.

We crashed. We killed a kid. The house had one of those things. They're building a big thing. We're riding these bikes.

"Cos, where are we going?" she asked.

"I don't know," he said. "Out of town, I guess."

She thought about that. *Okay, makes sense.*

"Cos, why did we crash?"

Silence.

"Cos, why did we crash?"

"I don't want to say," he said. "Probably just—probably just lost control. That's all."

Okay, makes sense.

In the back of her mind, she felt something walk in and close the door behind it. Her head hurt.

She pedaled harder.

A new voice appeared inside of her head. *Wren*, it called. It was warm. It sent hot chocolate cumshots dripping down the insides of her skull. Her breath hitched.

Who are you?

Sweat dripped from her brow. She watched her brother ahead of her. She tried to keep her focus on him, never looking away.

The voice spoke. *The name's Carmichael.*

THIRTY-SEVEN

There's nothing for you to do anymore. There's no fight worth fighting.

I'm going to tell you a story.

It's a story you know, because it's a story from your own life.

We open on a little girl who was so afraid to go to kindergarten. She'd never left home before. Never ever. She was pulling on her mother's dress, screaming. But mother needed her to go because she hadn't been working for so long and that her family really needed the money. So she drove her there and let her cry, she cried some too, but when it was time she let her go.

The little girl walked into the room and the teacher did that thing that all teachers do (believe me when I use the word all), when they kneel down to your level and talk all sweet-like. They love doing that shit. They love trying to make the best out of a bad thing.

Remember that moment, when you heard the door close behind you and your mother walking away. You saw the teacher's big eyes and her white teeth and the only thing you could think to do was open your little mouth and scream! You screamed! You batted at the teacher wildly with your tiny little baby fists and struck her again and again. Of course, it caused her no pain. You were just a little thing. But it did wipe the smirk off her face.

You stood there, your face all puffy—tears and snot slicking your face, and all the other kids were looking at you, staring at you like you were a wild animal. The teacher went to her desk and came back, with a more tentative kindness. "Good girls get cookies," she said.

"Cookies?"

"Yes, chocolate chip."

And then suddenly, there was peace. You ate the cookie.

Sweet, perfect.

You were docile. You colored quietly. You learned to spell. You sat in a line and said "yes, ma'am" and "no, ma'am." But we both know, underneath the mask of civility is chaos, violence.

We are removing decorum.

We are the primal force that earns cookies.

I can tell you more stories. I can tell you stories you've never heard. I can tell you futures you've never seen.

But first, you just have to help me. That's all. You have to help me.

How?

Up ahead, there's a sign. What does it say?

THIRTY-EIGHT

"Exit," said Wren. "The sign reads Exit."

Cossel slowed down. "What did you say?"

Wren pointed. "That sign says exit. But it's not normal, right? It's a special sign."

They were at an empty intersection, one road launching into the highway with an exit sign. Cossel squinted. *No, that's not entirely right.* The green sign had been painted over, adjusted in a small way. An arrow was drawn onto it, pointing away from the freeway, leading them to an empty right turn toward industrial Springfield.

"Hey, Wren," he said. "Do you remember that post? They said something about an exit, right? For those looking for resistance?"

He turned back to his sister, to see her gazing off into space, her eyes twitching back and forth.

"Shit, we need to get you help. How are you feeling?"

"Fine," she said. "Just tired."

He nodded. "Maybe they have some help, right?"

"Sure," she said, absently.

He started pedaling. Wren trailed behind him, turning in wide zig-zags down the street. He looked for any sign of people—normal people.

But the buildings were empty, or at least appeared to be. Brutalist, functionalist structures towered over him. All concrete and steel. Towers smoked but there was no hint of anyone inside of them making that smoke.

But then he caught sight of something. Graffiti. Fresh paint. White, dripping—the word EXIT and an arrow pointing down the road.

"You see that?" he asked. Cossel felt like he had to keep talking to his sister to keep her with him. He'd heard that somewhere, although he wasn't sure if it was true. Some concussion protocol he must've overheard during a school game. *But then again, if she's concussed, should she be riding a bike?*

Cossel felt helpless. He didn't know what to do. He was so close to feeling safe. But then everything went to shit.

The road seemed to elongate, but there were more arrows, more hastily graffitied EXITs to follow. He thought they might be getting close. Some of the paint still looked wet.

The next arrow made them take a turn. Up a hill that was nearly out of town. Everything was concrete and steel, but in between the factories, there were also small hole-in-the-wall diners, bass shops, and bars. For some reason, this comforted Cossel. He felt better now. This was a sign of life.

Halfway up the hill, a spray-painted EXIT pointed them toward a gap in a concrete wall. It led to a narrow alley that seemed remarkably clean to Cossel, who was used to cinematic visions of them—caked in trash and broken bottles.

"Stay with me, Wren. We're gonna find help."

"Yeah, I'm here, I'm good." She sounded dreamy, as if she were pedaling in two places at once.

The alley was all brick, a couple of heavy metal doors kept secrets. Another arrow pointed them forward. And they kept pedaling, Cossel looked around with eagle eyes to see some sign of safety—

And then he had it.

Up ahead.

A single word.

EXIT.

No arrow, just EXIT.

"Wren, it's just up ahead."

"Okay, okay."

Cossel threw the bike to the ground and stared at the lettering. The word EXIT stretched across an old wooden door that was missing a handle.

"What do we do?" he said aloud, knowing full well that Wren would be no help.

"Knock."

He did as she said.

They waited, listened.

But there was nothing, only silence.

"Open it," said Wren. "It's not locked."

"Are you feeling better?"

"I think so, yeah," she said.

"Okay."

Cossel pushed the door open and walked inside to an empty, dusty room.

Across from them was an old-timey elevator, the sort with the iron gates.

"Do you know how to use one of those?" asked Cossel.

"I'm sure we can figure it out," said Wren. Her voice was less distracted now, she seemed more put together.

Cossel let out a weak laugh as she moved the gate to the side and selected a floor. "Room stop spinning?" he asked.

"That's right," she said. "All better now."

"Good. I was afraid I was gonna lose you."

Wren didn't even need his help selecting the floor. There it was, marked with a crudely scratched EXIT.

"What's up here, do you think?"

"We'll find out," said Wren.

The elevator dinged. Cossel, instinctively, looked up to the ceiling. The ding echoed in such a way that he was pretty sure there was a physical bell directly above him.

In front of them, the door opened.

Through the bars, he saw a little over a dozen people. Most of them were dressed in everyday clothing, some of them in work clothes, some of them in sweats. One was leaning on the radiator and smoking out an open window. There were men, women, and a handful of children.

Wren reached for the gate.

A hand shot out. "Wait," it growled.

"We're normal," said Cossel. "We're normal."

"How did you find this place?"

Wren looked to Cossel and nodded.

"We followed the signs."

The voice's owner appeared in front of the gate. Small, flint-like eyes, a white mustache, his cheek and chin covered in short bristles. His hair was white too, pulled back in a ponytail. All the same, he was younger than his hair suggested. Cossel placed him as ten years older than his father.

"Have you been followed?"

"No. I don't think so," said Wren. "The streets are empty. It was just us."

"Most of them are probably helping with the building," said the white-haired man.

"You kids do the focus group thingie?"

Cossel nodded.

"Yeah, a lot of us did. Not all of us though. I didn't." He said it with a bit of weary pride.

"My sister hit her head," said Cossel. "Is anyone in there able to help her?"

Behind him, a woman craned her neck. "I'm a nurse."

"What are your names?" asked the man.

Cossel told them.

"Your sister's hurt?"

"Yes."

"Goddamnit." He sighed. Then, let go of the gate. "I'm Rod.

Not Roddy. Not Roderick. Just Rod. You're gonna wanna talk to Ella, over there. She'll take care of you."

Cossel and Wren left the elevator, stepping tentatively into a concrete loft. White light from the cracked windows poured in. Dust danced in the beams of light. People huddled in blankets, each of them a careful distance away from the next. They eyed them with unvarnished suspicion.

Rod said, "This is a secret place. We got to keep it a secret. Can't just let anyone in."

"We're not just anyone," said Wren.

Cossel darted an eye to his sister, unsure of what she meant.

The woman named Ella grabbed Wren by the arm and sat her down beside her. "Where are your parents?" she asked.

"They're gone," said Cossel.

She frowned. "I'm sorry. You poor things. You both need to rest. It won't fix anything, but it's nice to not have to think for a minute, right?"

"I'm okay," said Cossel. "For now, anyway. Thanks." Still, despite his protest, he yawned.

She shined her phone flashlight into Wren's eyes. "Yeah, that's good at least. Eyes are acting normal. Are you dizzy?"

Wren thought for a moment. "No."

"No? Not at all?"

"Not at all."

"Good. That's good. You're probably okay, but for the sake of your brain, don't sleep for the next twelve hours, okay?"

"Okay," said Wren.

Ella looked at them with a sort of motherly concern. "Do you need some food?"

Cossel shook his head. "I'm not hungry."

"Me neither," said Wren.

"Just let me know," said Ella. She closed her eyes. "This has been crazy, right?"

"What do you know? What's happening?"

She sighed. "They've been changing people. Or maybe not changing them—have you ever cooked? Do you watch cooking shows?"

"I've seen one or two," lied Cossel.

"Well, you know how in the shows they always reduce sauces? Cook 'em down until they're sweet and thick? Well, I think that's what they've been doing to folks here. They've been cooking them down. That's what happened to me." She blinked away a tear. "All I wanted was some money. They offered me $100,000 and I was so burnt out from Covid and everything, you know? It just never got better. They offered me so much and I couldn't resist. It was just me and my husband and my little girl."

Why'd she get offered more? he wondered.

Cossel swallowed. He didn't have to ask to know why they weren't here today. Instead, he asked, "How did you break free of it? My Mom—I think she was able to break free of it. Become, uh, un-reduced. At least for a couple minutes. It came in waves for me too. Sometimes I couldn't think at all. I felt like my impulses were all off. Sometimes, I felt this wave of shame, of disgust at whatever I was doing."

She nodded. "That's how it is for a lot of us. We all have something that clicks us out. It's different for everyone. For me, it was when my husband… my husband prepared dinner and I realized the baby wasn't crying anymore." A hard, coughing sob erupted from her mouth. "That's when I broke the Product."

Cossel didn't know what to do. He looked to his sister, but she remained frozen. He wasn't sure if she was even listening. "I'm sorry," he said. "I'm so sorry." He patted her on the back.

She touched his hand in return and the small blossom of warmth that came from it was a welcome feeling. These moments of connection were what he had missed, they were the cement that was boiled out of the sauce.

"How did everyone find each other?"

Ella shook her head. She pointed to Rod. "That's him. Rod, tell him about this place."

Rod was sitting on the floor, in a nest made of sleeping bags, reading. He looked up from his book and said, raising his voice slightly. "I've been following C/C for the last year," he said. "I was the first to know about them. I was the first to come here and try to tell people. Their shit doesn't stick to me, for whatever reason. I don't know why. I think it's because I'm already insane, already a dropout. I've never held a job and never learned the value of money. I barter and wander and live on streets and tents and garden my own food. Cormorant doesn't know what to do with people like me."

Wren said, "They can kill you though, right?"

Cossel looked at his sister, the words came out of her lips like ice.

"They can try. They have before. But they haven't been able to get the job done, for whatever reason."

"They've done this before?" asked Cossel.

"Sure, yeah. On a smaller scale, of course. Nothing this big. I saw Mr. Cormorant doing his act down south, sort of a tent revival type thing for young capitalists. He'd put his hand on these *Wolf of Wall Street* wannabes and then whisper in their ear and they'd come out saying that it was a revelation. They were in the palm of his hand. He did that a couple of times. It was mostly harmless then. He was a weird guy with precise insight. I went to one because there was a deli tray. I saw the flyer and it said there'd be food, which was enough for me at the time. I was used to showing up to events, entirely shameless, and eating their food. So, I went. I watched all these motherfuckers get up and ask questions about sales, consumers, and marketing and realized that this was some Mecca for business gurus. Cormorant did his song and dance and talked a lot about what makes people, well, people. That was his whole pitch—to reach down into the fundamentals of time, space, and life itself and figure out what makes people tick. Of course, these guys ate it all up. I watched from the back, filling myself with sandwich meat. At the end of it, Cormorant makes a beeline for me, and I try to get away but can't. He comes up and touches me and for a moment I just blacked out. The world literally dimmed and the only thing I could see was him and his black eyes. He towered over me and he looked so smug, so purely evil. And then, when he let go, he made this sort of thin frown. He said, 'I suppose I have nothing to offer you,' and walked away. But after that, the whole night over, I was shitting bricks, man. I'd never seen anything like that. Who *has* seen anything like that? I couldn't stop thinking about that because I figured he might as well have been the devil. The real life, actual devil. And when you see a real fuckin' devil—and yeah, I can't call him a man, because really, I don't think he is one. I think he's an *entity* or something like that. Like, a demon, some archetype outside the realm of humanity. You can't help but want to keep tabs on someone like that. From the guru seminars, he started doing small product unveilings. Prototypes of what he brought you guys. He finds people to do his *bidding*. Like a vampire from the old movies. He chews them up and spits them out."

"He did that to a… friend of mine. Dom. He was helping him. Was his assistant or something. I heard he died."

"A kid, right?" said Rod. He looked into his nest, fumbling for a piece of paper. "Yeah, Dominic. We know about him. Sorry for your loss. When these people spend enough time under the Product, they've shed every societal construct they've ever learned—good and bad. This isn't just stop at the red light stuff, it's also stuff like don't murder, rape, and steal. Enough time with the Product fucks your head up so bad that you're nothing more than primal urges. A base layer. The difference between Cormorant and myself is that Cormorant believes that this base layer, this unbridled desire to consume, *is* humanity. If it is, I don't wanna play the game."

Cossel had not reached the phase of teenager-dom where he played with existentialist thought and big questions. He wanted a car. He wanted to have sex. He wanted his peers to like him. But even he realized that all of the things he wanted were still *wants*. The thought of being absent from these, made him wonder if he had a personality to begin with, or if he was just a conglomeration of wants.

"They're building a tower. A bigger version of the Product," he said.

Rod nodded. "Yes. He's recruited a lot of the town to help. They're not like the others though. They still have their minds, more or less. The rest of them are a chosen secondary class, hoping to rule over those yapping ids, or something. Cormorant offers money, riches, whatever it takes to get you into his web. And now he's got a lot of people building a tower and they don't even realize that it's going to enslave them too. Scramble them up into the same hungry mouths."

Cossel shook his head. "I guess I just don't understand why. Why would he want this? He can't profit off of it, can he?"

"It's a philosophical mission," added Wren, her eyes cold and distant.

"I don't know, maybe," said Rod. "Why does the scorpion sting the frog? It's just something scorpions do. We don't know why Mr. Cormorant wants to do the things he does, but his internal machinations make it so that he does do them and we're the ones who have to stop him."

"Stop him?"

Rod smiled broadly. He gestured to the other end of the loft. Plastic-wrapped piles of what looked like off-white Play-Doh stood. "That's C4," he said. "We're going to end this bullshit tonight. We're going to all go out tonight, as a team, and blow up his fucking tower. We're gonna blow up his minions. We're gonna try to bring them back to something like sanity. But most of all, we're going to kill Mr. Cormorant."

Rod spoke with such fury that Cossel couldn't help but be swept up in his words.

But then, his sister spoke. "No, Rod. I don't think that will happen. But it is nice to see you *wanting*."

THIRTY-NINE

The air left the room.

Cossel looked to his sister and suddenly found he didn't recognize her.

Rod stood up with a hammer (*no not the hammer*) gathered from his things and made a beeline for Wren as soon as she spoke.

He had it lifted in the air, he was going to bring it down on her face and he did—he slammed the hammer through Wren's face and blood came down. It punched a hole through her skull and he reared back and slammed it in again, this time breaking off another continent of bone and nailing shards of it into her brain. Wren staggered back, her hands raised in the air, straight out, like Frankenstein's monster.

But still, she stood.

"Tear her to fucking bits!" screamed Rod.

But no one knew what to do. Few were accustomed to enacting violence so quickly. These were parents, children, nurses—regular people. Never had they been called to spring to the ready and kill someone before. So, they hesitated. They stood in place, their mouths agape, and watched Wren steady herself from the impact.

Cossel was just like them. Scared, confused. He was about to jump into the fray, to tackle Rod and save his sister. He planted his feet into the cement, steadied himself, and was about to lunge, when his knee slipped out of place. *Fuck*. He adjusted himself. The knee went back into place, and he started moving one foot in front of the other, very careful to lift his feet high up off the ground so that he would not trip on his drop foot. But by the time he had made it to where he was standing, Rod had already been thrown across the room, his body folded like a collapsible chair—the back of his head to his heels. He gurgled blood and the top half of him broke out into shivers before his snapped form lay still forever.

Cossel turned toward Wren. She was not Wren.

She *looked* like Wren—mostly. But she was not his sister. Her mouth hung open, as if the muscles and tendons that held her jaw in place had been neatly cut. Her new slack jaw led to a black hole. Her eyes had glassed over milky white. Her new pupil-less eyes were lined with black veins that crawled like photographic negatives of lightning strikes across her corneas.

"Wren?"

A deep, blubbering laugh came from within her. It sounded completely divorced from her vocal cords. It said, "I will lay waste to your revolutionary enclave like I have laid waste to lifeforms long forgotten."

Cossel backed up, he felt the cold concrete on his shoulders. His hands searched for the iron gate.

Then, the people behind the Wren Thing acted.

There were only about thirteen of them, but it was as if something snapped inside of them. Rod's last words came to them, albeit late, and they started rushing toward the Wren Thing. One man grabbed her from behind, placing her in a chokehold. The nurse, Ella, screeched like a banshee and grabbed her legs. More came at her, more hands fell on her body and suddenly the Wren Thing did not seem so destructive.

They tore at her like animals.

Cossel, now that she was on the floor, turned to the elevator, he threw the gate open and pressed the button. That same echoey bell chimed and he looked back eagerly, shifting his weight. *I need to get the fuck out of here*, he thought.

The Wren Thing was on the ground. Low, hellish bellows emanated from her insides, but now they were holding parts of her down while yanking on her arms. Their faces had become ravenous, twisted in a sort of hungry rage that Cossel found difficult to witness.

One limb came loose with the help of a knife. Ella sawed the skin around the shoulder joint while a line of survivors played tug-of-war with Wren's arm.

Pop.

They fell back and the Wren Thing howled in pain.

Blood dumped out of her in buckets, slicking the floor with the red.

Ding.

Cossel turned back, ready to dive into the elevator.

The doors opened and he stopped.

No.

Mr. Cormorant stood in the elevator, his red lips pursed as if he were about to lean in for a kiss.

Cossel's heart dropped into his stomach.

"Cossel," he said. "You left early."

"Y—yes."

Mr. Cormorant leaned to the side, looking past him to the Wren Thing being torn apart. "It's no use," he said. "You cannot kill that which does not live. Carmichael, show them."

The people stopped dead in their tracks. The Wren Thing writhed like a salted slug for a few minutes. Then, she stayed still.

Bones cracked. Cossel heard wet sloshing sounds within her. She sat up.

Everyone else, all those others lured here by the promise of an Exit, backed up to the walls of the loft.

The Wren Thing's skin *boiled*. Flesh popped and sizzled, fat cooked within her own body. Whatever was inside of her was turning her muscles into meat, cooking her in her own fat. Cossel imagined the pain she must be in.

But the Wren Thing showed no signs of pain, there was no agony in those white eyes.

The arm too, the one separated from her body and spurting blood on the floor also began to boil and cool in its place, before charring and flaming.

The heat had by now dried out Wren's flesh (*my sister*) and was beginning to crack, smoke, and burn as well.

Cossel watched his sister burst into flames. As his sister was engulfed in red, orange, and white energy, three words seared themselves into his mind.

I am alone.

"Wren!" he shouted.

"No," said Mr. Cormorant. "No longer Wren."

He was right too. Wren was gone. The flames were no longer in a Wren shape. In fact, the flames themselves had settled. Cossel felt the warm heat of the orb's energy. Meanwhile, the arm—now a smaller orb of energy—had lifted itself off the floor and joined the floating nebula.

Mr. Cormorant walked to the middle of the loft, where the scared people were now his audience.

The elevator door closed.

A soft, comforting heat emanated from the center of the room.

The light of the thing burned his eyes.

"May I introduce you to my partner, Carmichael," said Mr. Cormorant. "We have been in business a very long time. And we will be in business for many more years in the future, I assure you. Carmichael, please, make your pitch."

The orb glowed and began to move. It was roughly the size of a large man's torso, but Cossel was sure that size was no matter for it. That it could be as small as it wanted, or as large. It circled the room, sizzling through the air, engulfing one person after another. Cossel expected them to burst into flames, but instead, their faces were overtaken by shock, then abject terror, and then finally, melancholy placidity.

Cossel closed his eyes when the ball named Carmichael came for him, but it did not matter if he saw it or not. It swallowed him all the same.

FORTY

This all happened in an instant.

But for Cossel, time was a distant memory. Carmichael swallowed him and the only thing he saw was a blinding light, and then: *black*.

He was cold. The sound of harsh winds blowing across unfamiliar landscapes threatened to collapse his eardrums. "Where are we?"

The beginning.

The voice was calm, kind. His inflection was that of a trusted teacher who had graduated into trusted confidant. It was a voice Cossel recognized, but had not heard in a long time.

"Dad?"

No, but I sound like him, don't I? I can also sound like your mother. Your friends. Your sister. Yourself. I chose your father at Mr. Cormorant's request though. He thinks it'll be the best thing for you right now.

"Who are you?"

I am the glue that binds all things living. I am a representative of the food chain. Anytime you hear about dog-eat-dog or climbing to the top, hunting, killing, eating, making more of something, taking it from others—that's me.

"Who is Mr. Cormorant?"

A gifted liaison.

"Are you his boss?"

In some ways, yes. But I prefer to say we are partners.

"So, you can kill him?"

I can do whatever I want to, anything.

"Please," Cossel screamed, above the howling winds. "Kill him! Kill him!"

I don't think that I will. We are on twin missions. We are proselytizing what is natural, what is base—the fundamental mechanics of nature. Consumption.

Cossel did not know what to say, instead, he tried to hold himself in the darkness.

Let me help you understand, it said. *You are cold now. Let me warm you. And in return for my warmth, you can give me your life. It's that easy.*

The orb illuminated and the sky filled with burning light. He was lying down on a rocky surface, somewhere infinite and harsh. Red swirls of dust jousted in the distance.

"Where am I?" he screamed.

You already asked that.

Cossel thought, he breathed. He tried to calm himself. He tried not to think about how alone he was, how infinitely alone he would be for the rest of his life.

No more questions. I'm going to show you something.

Cossel blinked and reality had warped. Carmichael carried him along through time and space. The world was black now, it was truly at the beginning. Then, a violent explosion. A great, powerful force. A billion nuclear explosions that were so vast that they would've swallowed everything.

This is the beginning, said Carmichael. *This is where everything began. Right here. Do you like it? It's pretty, right? I always thought so. I like searching through time and seeing these moments again and again. Large doesn't do it justice, does it? Who would've thought that so much could come from something as banal as violence? But it did. And I think that's important to remember. Even now.*

Cossel felt behind him, he felt for the earth. He grabbed a handful. It didn't feel right. It felt metallic, a different cold.

Reality changed again. What was large was now small. He was a microscope, staring at a tiny wriggling form.

This is the universe. I bet you didn't think it was alive. But yes, it was. For a very long time, it was. It is a nameless thing. And it grew, very large in fact. In fact, you could say that for a time, it was the universe.

Cossel now saw the thing, a snippet of the beast. His mind threatened to snap under the weight. He reached out to touch its colorless skin, warm and breathing in and out. The blood inside it raged. The thing sounded like war.

The thing was very large, as you can see. But, one day, it came to its natural end. There was no grand murder or horrendous cancer. It just was what it was. Things live and then they die. That is the way life happens, even in the beginning. But for us, and for you, life didn't truly begin till the First died. Its body decayed and is still decaying, and from this natural celestial rot, everything else came after. Stars, planets, gravity, life—all of it born from the rotting corpse of the First thing that ever lived.

He reached his hand back again to see if he could feel that metallic touch of *something. I'm not here, I'm in the loft. I'm not here, I'm somewhere else.*

Carmichael said, *I too was born from this great decay. If you look very closely, you can still see the beast floating around. I am just one of many maggots. And we have evolved as predator and—*

His hand latched on to something. He pulled.

And suddenly, the cold winds disappeared. The stars were gone. The infinite expanse of the First thing was gone, and the bright light of Carmichael shined bright in his eyes.

The bell sounded.

A perfect sound.

The orb kept talking, its voice filled his head.

This decay will take millennias to cease, it said.

But Cossel wasn't listening. He was watching Mr. Cormorant.

He tried to keep his mind clear, in case Carmichael would realize he was not with him in the cosmic coffin of the great progenitor.

Half of them were already gone, devoured. Mr. Cormorant had unhinged his jaw to the floor, revealing a maw of bone shards and undulating pink flesh. He grabbed Ella, the nurse, and he was tempted to scream out, but couldn't. He stood behind her and simply rocked her back and forth, forward and backward, then tipped her so that her head rested in his mouth. His mouth closed around her and he reared his head back. He pulverized her, somehow. His black shark eyes stared at the ceiling, seeing nothing—perhaps. He was going through each one, devouring them. When Ella was gone, there was a child.

Mr. Cormorant was not around at the very beginning, but he was at the second beginning. He is my son, which means you could say this is a family business.

Cossel darted as quickly as he could into the elevator.

FORTY-ONE

He expected to be chased. As soon as the elevator doors opened, he ran. He shook off the scent of rot, he let Carmichael's words slip out of his mind, and he picked up the bike he left leaning on the brick wall, and began pedaling furiously.

No screams. No calls for him to stop. There was nothing.

His lungs were tired and ragged, and he was sure that he was being watched, followed. But nothing touched his mind, nothing touched him.

Streets passed him by. Springfield wasn't large, but it was bigger than he thought.

Sometimes, he'd stop, cough his lungs out and look behind him. The great Product loomed.

And then he'd get back on his bike and keep pedaling.

Everyone was gone.

He made it to the freeway, somehow. But he was still a boy, he was not far out of town. He could not get very far without a vehicle. It was very cold. He figured if he could see at all he'd be able to see his breath. The warmth felt good on his fingers, the warmth of his insides.

The best thing about seeing nothing was not seeing the Product.

The freeway cut through mountainous wilds. He rolled his bike up a narrow hiking trail into the trees. He gasped as he made it up the side. His feet slipped on loose rocks, and he fell forward on stinging palms, cursing under his breath. He protected his knee from impact though. He knew if his knee went, this escape meant nothing.

He held himself under a tree, barely visible in the light of the moon.

Cossel closed his eyes and dreamed of nothing good. Nothing good at all. Mouths. Thousands of hungry mouths.

He shivered. He woke at dawn. He had not slept well. Cossel thought he was further from the freeway than he was, but when he looked out he had only made it about fifty feet before collapsing.

He looked at his stolen bike, measuring it with his eyes. It would not last forever. It would get a flat, the chain would break. Bikes needed maintenance. He would continue on though.

On the road, cars whooshed past him, blowing his messy brown hair into his eyes. He knew he was comically close to his own home, despite how much his body ached from effort. Thirty? Forty miles?

At best.

But he passed signs for Springfield, and it gradually disappeared further and further into the distance.

A town was coming up. A small one, one smaller than Springfield. He wondered if they had a bus station. He had money, he could go far away.

Asheville.

The sign said that 5,361 people called it their home. Cossel didn't think he'd be one of them, but by the time he arrived, the bike was gone. It was in a ditch somewhere, miles back—two flat tires. He walked into town, looking dirty and tired. Sweat made his clothes stick to him.

An impotent sun hung above his head. He didn't like to look at it. It reminded him of Carmichael.

He stopped at a corner store and grabbed a bottle of water. The cashier said, "You been traveling?"

Cossel nodded.

"From where?"

"Aways away."

The cashier smiled. His eyes were black, like that of a shark. He motioned to the bottle. "Will that be cash or card?"

Cossel swallowed. "Cash."

When the car stopped on the road, Cossel felt a leap of joy. He'd been walking for two hours, his thumb in the air the whole time. The air was dusty and cold. He was tired. Hungry.

Cossel approached the window.

The driver craned his neck. He looked normal enough. About his father's age. Short beard, glasses, dressed in a flannel. His car was clean.

"Aren't you a bit young to be hitchhiking?"

"I'm not that young," said Cossel. He'd decided that answer would be best earlier. He'd played this conversation out in his head while running away.

"Where are you going?" There was genuine concern in the man's voice.

Cossel shrugged. "Anywhere, I guess."

"Well, I'm going to Boise. Is that alright?"

"Yeah, that's fine with me. Anywhere is great."

"Alright, kid. Get in. You hungry?"

"I can eat."

The man nodded. "Yeah, I thought so. I think there's a burger place up ahead. Maybe we can grab a bite. I'm buying."

The man's name was Greg. He was a high school teacher, visiting his sister in Boise. He insisted on driving everywhere because he felt a sense of connection and longing for monotony.

"There's something beautiful about it, you know? The scenery. The adventures. The pit stops."

But Cossel couldn't think about any of that, his hunger was so great. Cossel bit into his burger, felt the juices flooding down his chin. He swallowed. "This tastes so good."

"It *is* good," said the man. "It's perfect. It's maybe the most perfect thing ever made. It's an American Cheeseburger."

Cossel laughed. He mulled over the words. "An *American* cheeseburger," he repeated.

Greg smiled. He ran a hand through his hair. "That's right. This American Cheeseburger is maybe the most important thing you'll ever eat, ever see. Wanna know why?"

"Sure, hit me."

Greg cracked his knuckles. He lifted the bun off the top of the burger. "Well, first, let's just admire the bun here. This isn't just a bun, Cossel. This is a symbol. This is a symbol of agriculture. This is *wheat*. This is the stuff we grew so we wouldn't have to keep moving from place to place. This is part of the DNA of the American Cheeseburger. It's the past, looking toward the future. Look at this thing. Perfectly molded into this half dome. Dotted with sesame seeds that might as well be the stars we see. Look at the color. Browned, inviting, toasted. Now, look at what's just below it—tomato, lettuce, onion, pickle. This is color. This is life. But it's also a perfunctory statement. No one thinks a burger is healthy because of the vegetables on it. But we see the vegetables and we feel better about it anyway. Do you understand what I'm saying, Cossel? This element adds a textural crunch, but it also adds a visual signpost—this is okay, keep doing it." Greg moved the lettuce, tomato, onion, and pickles aside. "Now right here though, this is truly what I love. It's why I call it an American Cheeseburger, although I'm not sure why I would think it could be anything else. See this here? This yellow square? This right here is your birthright. This is where agriculture has taken you. From crops to processed cheese. Some will say this cheese is false, that it is bad cheese because it is made in a factory and choked with preservatives, but I'd be hard-pressed to find a more perfect cheese for an American Cheeseburger. It melts evenly. It falls apart. It becomes the glue that ties everything together—forever and ever.

"But the cheese is not the main course. It's what it covers. The meat. Beef, cow. Death itself. We are eating death and therefore we are demonstrating mastery over life. We are taking death and grinding it up. Reforming it so that it becomes something new. A patty. A shape pleasing to us and our mouths."

Greg put the burger back together. He took a bite. "And how could we not want one of these? They're a mix of the organic and plastic. Old, new, and iconoclastic. They fill us up, they sustain us, and they also communicate to us that we have a home. This is an American Cheeseburger, after all. It is more than its parts. More than preservatives, agriculture, and death. It is a symbol of who and what we are."

Greg licked his red lips. Cossel sat dazed, his pupils shaking.

"And I only have one question, Cossel—would you like another?"

FORTY-TWO

Cossel woke on a Saturday morning, sun streaming through the window. He got up fast, terrified for a reason he couldn't understand. Somewhere, there was a sound. A loud wind, blowing—an exotic hum. But in moments, it vanished. Or, rather, bled into the background of the noises of a normal house on a normal Saturday.

The TV was on downstairs.

He got up unsteadily and ran downstairs. A strange urgency overtook him that he couldn't explain. *Is something wrong?*

There was nothing wrong.

On the steps, his heart skipped a beat and he found himself looking at his feet, but he couldn't figure out *why* he was looking at his feet.

He was looking to look, he guessed.

Downstairs, his father flipped through channels, bored. His mother sat on a bar stool and flipped through Instagram.

"Where's Wren?" he asked.

"At work," said Ed.

"She's always working," said Vee. "She's smart. I got to work later. Maybe I can get a couple more hours or something."

Ed nodded. "That'd be nice. We could use the money."

They noticed Cossel standing at the foot of the stairs, his mouth agape. "Something wrong, kid?"

"I think I had a bad dream," he said.

"Welcome to my life," said Vee, laughing too loud.

Cossel chuckled uncomfortably. He said, "Is everything alright?"

Ed shrugged. "Same as always, I suppose. You okay?"

He shook his head, frantically. "Fine, fine." When his parents did not cease their staring, he said, quickly, "I'm going to go for a walk."

"Alright," said Vee. "Be careful."

Cossel went outside.

The sun was bright and there was a faint, cold burning smell in the air. He breathed deep and it soon vanished.

He walked and ran and kept asking himself: *is something wrong here, there has to be something wrong?*

But nothing was wrong. Nothing was wrong at all.

Although, sometimes, when he blinked, he saw the image of a great tower on the horizon—black and grim and all-consuming. And sometimes when he blinked twice, he saw more of them being built. But that was fine, he would just blink less.

He was going to buy a car soon, that much he knew. He would buy it tomorrow, because he'd saved up money for it. The used car would make Grady weep. Grady would cry, just like the time that his mother tore his fucking guts out in a pile on the kitchen floor.

In bed, at night, Cossel learned to become accustomed to normality. Everything slipped away from him like a bad dream. It was gone. Vanished. It slipped away like sand in an hourglass. Even when he heard words in his head, those were gone too.

When the voice would tell him to go to Wren's room, the words evaporated by the time his hand was on the doorknob.

He would buy his car and then he would find new things to buy, because that is what was necessary.

At the bus stop one day, he saw a red-lipped man. Rotund with a white face, like stage makeup white. He was wearing a tuxedo and Mickey Mouse gloves. Cossel felt a warm glow in his chest. "Do I know you?" he asked.

The man smiled and said, "I know *you*."

And then he got on the bus and left, for somewhere else, he supposed. Or maybe not. Cossel couldn't keep the thought in his mind. It was a squirrelly thought. It weaseled in and out of his grasp whenever he tried to wrestle it. He chalked it up to being normal, average. *That's just the kind of guy I am, I guess. Average. Average guys have bad memories.*

In his bed, or in Wren's bed, or in his parent's bed between them—his body rocking between theirs—he sometimes reached out behind him and felt something black and cold and harsh. A wind blew through his hair, and he smelled the inexplicable scent of rot. But then, it went. Just as everything else. There was a hum. And then, there wasn't.

He thought to himself, *I need to buy a car.*